LOVE LOCKED IN

TISHA ANDREWS

Hebrews 11:1

Faith is the substance of things hoped for, the evidence of things not seen.

Synopsis

Faith is to have complete trust or confidence in someone or something designed to love, protect, and honor you. That is a perfect description of Faith, the eldest daughter of Pastor Theodore Valentine. She has complete trust in the first man she loved, her father, who selfishly puts his own needs, saturated with greed, over his child.

While Faith desires to minister to the people of God through music, her heart opens up and wide for Denver Daniels, a rough around the edges yet honorable young man who attends her church. With a first name like Faith and a last name like Valentine, Denver knows everything he desires and needs is deposited into one girl, and he has to have her. What starts out as a simple crush evolves into a forever love, or so they hope, until someone else who has eyes for Faith interferes.

Raziel "Razz" Streeter, like Faith, has a love for music that soon catapults his otherwise dark life into a space of light. That light is Faith. With the help of her father, Razz's desperate need to be validated costs Faith not only her first love but herself, being sucked into their world of selfishness and greed.

Once the foundation of Faith's life is shaken and secrets are revealed, a getaway to Mason yields as more than a time to hide. It births a second chance for Faith to love again when she reconnects with her first love—Denver. While Denver struggles to forgive, Faith's presence unlocks the love he has deeply tucked deep away in his heart for her, and he just can't seem to let go. Even if that means revealing more secrets that could destroy them all.

Preface

I am so excited to have penned my sixth book under B. Love Publications and even more excited that I get to share it with you. The beauty of this one is me creating more love and magic in the city of Mason. You first were introduced to Mason in my holiday novel, *Noel: Stay Another Day*, where Knight and Noel meet and fall in love. They're back and so are my hero and heroine, Denver and Faith, who've reconnected years later. With this read, you experience a budding, young-adult romance before life takes them down a tumultuous trail of deceit and betrayal.

Having said that, the first few chapters are a reflection of that time in their lives, but once they reconnect, it is on from there. Trust me. Their story becomes one full of drama, sexual tension, intimacy, and most definitely, love… a second chance love at that!

As always, my stories are penned with a focus on a redemption. That means the characters are flawed, making poor choices either intentionally or unintentionally, yet may have a chance to redeem those poor choices through the channel of love.

If you can rock with that and experience this journey the way that Denver and Faith spoke to me, keep reading! And when you are done reading, please be so kind as to leave me an honest review.

Your takeaway of what they created through me makes me better.

On that note, welcome back!

Locked Love In

A NOVEL BY

Tisha Andrews

Prologue

The rhythm of her heart sped up as he brushed his lips across hers. Lips thick and full that made Faith want to die right there right then as Denver took her mouth. She closed her eyes as she savored the taste. It was a mixture of mint and what he had smoked, so intense and intoxicating she felt her center pulsating.

"Tell me what you want from me 'cause anything you want, anything you need, I'll kill to give that shit to you," he said with conviction, gripping her neck as she slid underneath him.

She spread her thighs open, allowing him to have a full view of her perfectly shaven pussy as her robe fell open. She never knew exposing herself would be so powerful, so ardent as he whispered, "Stop holding back from me, ma."

He slipped one finger in between her fattened, pinkish brown folds that seemed to have bloomed just for him. Her swollen nub quivered as he bent down and blew on it, causing her to hiss as her back arched. The touch of his fingers to her sex sent her into a frenzy, his calloused fingers strumming on her love that tucked and pulled at her soul.

Tears spilled down the side of her temple coupled with sweat that rained down her body, a sweat he'd worked up simply by being in her presence. It was like that with them, always like that. Things were never cold or lukewarm. They were hot, very hot to the point they felt they were about to combust and explode.

"I wanna suck on this pussy until the sun comes up and keep going until that motherfucker goes down," he hissed huskily, working her center as she released unintelligible pleas of pleasure. The declaration of what he desired to do to her was mind boggling as she chanted a foreign language of love, a language for his ears and heart only as she panted.

"Please," she begged, her chest heaving up and down when he sat up on his haunches, a mischievous smile appearing as he took her in. He was beyond in love, his eyes consumed by her mocha-colored breasts with areolas that peaked with excitement. "Don't… don't stop," she pleaded, missing his touch when he slid his two fingers in his mouth and sucked and pulled on them slowly.

"So fucking sweet, ma," he said, issuing that same smile as she tried to touch herself. He growled, slapping her hand away before he quickly lifted both of her thighs and rested his face in between her legs. "Hi, pretty pussy," he whispered against her as Faith released a loud wail, shaking her head. This was torture, pure torture, and she wanted it, needed it. When he softly blew inside of her love, her body quickly rose up. Her feet firmly planted on each side of his body as she rested on the palms of her hands looking down at him.

His peanut butter colored skin glistened, his soft brown eyes an anchor pulling her in as he pecked her center, then slowly drew circles around it as she cried out, "Please, noooo. Oh, fuck!"

He chuckled. "Naw, don't plead now," he spoke against her pussy before using his tongue to flick on the tip of her clitoris as her body ignited with a raging passion she couldn't contain. She belted out a loud wail deep from her belly, one he prayed he would fill up for her to release his children, his legacy.

"Yeah, say that shit, baby," he urged her. He then slid his stiffened tongue into her love, sliding in and out as she wound her hips. She panted while confessions of her need for more escaped from her lips, pouty lips Denver couldn't wait to have wrapped around his dick.

His tongue stroked her pussy like a hungry, starved savage. Up and down then 'round and around as she fed him the sweetest pussy on this side of heaven. Just when she was close to coming undone, he latched onto her swollen nub. Faith's eyes shot open, her lips quivering as he slowly and gently massaged her love with his tongue until her body gave way.

"Fuck, baby!" she bellowed, her pussy quaking all over his mouth.

"This my shit, Mouse. Always," he whispered ever so softly, pecking it a few times as she hummed and chanted even more. She gave him that ugly cry, that cry that came when it hurt so good and damn it, it felt better than good.

It was perfect. Perfect just like Faith, his Mouse.

"So fucking beautiful," he whispered to her then looked back down at his personal playground between her legs. "Thank you, pretty pussy," he spoke into her center, smiling. That made Faith laugh.

"Ugh, I hate you," she told him, shaking her head while relishing in the sight of his mouth covered and glistening from her release.

"The fuck you do." He laughed before he latched onto her pussy again, and she screamed.

"I have to stop this," she whispered to herself as she awakened before she realized she wasn't alone, screaming. "Joy! What the heck are you doing standing there?" she belted when she realized it was all a dream.

"No, hoe. Don't you be screaming at me. I told you to go and get your man. Fuck Razz. Never should have married him in the first place. Now what you need me to do? I got connections. Want me to call in a few favors, help you become a widow?" she posed, smiling and sipping on a mimosa at six in the morning. "Have some?"

"Trust me, he's not worth it," she huffed, flopping back on the bed as she covered herself up. "And no thank you. It's too early to start drinking, getting all numb. Shoot, that's the problem. I've been living my life numb," she admitted for the first time out loud.

"Girl, a little mimosa ain't never hurt nobody. Pastor got y'all thinking everything is a sin," she said, watching Faith toss a pillow over her face. "All the while, your husband is passing out penis like food stamps, except the hoes he chooses don't even qualify. I never liked that girl, sissy," Joy said, taking a seat next to her on the bed. "Now about all that moaning and hollering you was just doing."

"Did that really happen?" Faith asked her, close to tears, feeling the stickiness between her legs.

"It sure the hell did, but riddle me this. Why now? Because your bitch ass husband is cheating, or you've been stepping out too on that bootleg ass marriage?" Joy probed, pursing her lips.

"I have no clue what you're talking about," she said, quickly snatching the pillow from over her face with bucked eyes. "Can you just leave, Joy? I don't have time for this right now."

"Uh, last I checked, this is my place," Joy quipped, sipping her mimosa before she stopped and popped her lips.

"I don't know why I even came here," Faith groaned, rolling on her side.

"Hoe, because you know I'm the only one that won't judge you for leaving. You should have been left. Now the question is what's next? And I don't give a shit if you did buy this place; it's mine," she added. "Don't be no Indian giver, Faith."

"You think I want to stay here? Please," she said, looking over her shoulder. "I just know I wasn't staying with him."

"Him as in your husband?"

"Him as in Razz. You know what?" she said, sitting up and pulling her sheet over her body. "I feel like my entire life is a lie right now. Seven years' worth of lies I didn't create and I didn't even ask for. Then to mess it all up for Amber? How in the hell you cheat on your wife with the hair and makeup girl?"

"All pussy is pink, sissy," Joy said with a smile, something their grandmother, may God rest her soul, often said about their trifling pastor of a father. "And maybe it has been, but guess what?" she said, placing her glass down on the dresser. "You live to see another day and to start another life. Not everyone gets a second chance… with their first love," she told her, resting on the bed next to her sister as they both looked up at the ceiling. "Tried reaching out to him?"

"Uh, you forgot? That man went to prison and cut me off." She laughed, which was short-lived as she fought hard not to cry. "Did all of that just to get me caught up in him then turn around and dismiss me like I was the one that screwed up," she released, feeling herself get emotional all over again.

She'd been crying for days, indicated by her puffy red eyes and swollen nose.

"Then just start over period, *for yourself*. No men at all. And do it on your terms, Faith. Not mines, not Mama's, and definitely not Pastor. In fact, fuck Pastor. Do you," she spat, sucking her teeth.

"He's still our father." Faith sighed.

"He is, but guess what? He was when he made you get married and the one that still hasn't whooped your husband's ass. No, instead he's been grinning and smiling for the cameras while singing praises about his daughter, the great Faith Streeter and her husband, Razz. Girl, bye. Daddy's been using y'all while you've been lacking the right kind of love and being dick deprived. Now if anything is a sin, it's that shit right there," she said, snickering as Faith fought hard not to laugh, especially since she and Razz hadn't been intimate in more than six months. Even when they were, it wasn't much to brag about, but she'd never tell. She dismissed what they lacked in love and intimacy, throwing all of her energy into their successful music career.

Their life as a gospel and R and B duo team was demanding, beyond recording in the studio and performing in arenas all over the world. In between that, they had to promote, do interviews, and even negotiate endorsements and contracts like producers clawing at them from *Bravo* to shoot a reality show, *In the Streets with the Streeters.*

"And tell me how is it that you know that I've been dick deprived?" she asked, pursing her lips.

"Shoot, you have to be after what I heard. Oh fuck, Denver. Please fuck me," Joy mimicked, as Faith scrunched up her face that was flushed.

"Dang, sissy. I sounded like that?"

"Uh, yeah. Like I said, dick deprived," she emphasized with a smirk. "I guess money or the love of it can make you a fool sometimes. But here's one Valentine girl that will be her own cupid compliments of dildos, vibrators, and anal bullets. Fuck all that."

"You think Daddy's been using me?" Faith whispered, knowing the lengths he'd go to keep Piney Grove Ministries in the face of the people, televised all over the world.

"I *know* Daddy had his hand in that. Girl, you couldn't even stand Razz, and now here you are, hiding with the black sheep of the family. Hell, it can't get any worse than that if you let Pastor tell it. But it's whatever. I'm living my truth, Faith Caroline," she said, adding her middle name as she took her sister's hand.

"Alright now, Joy Elaine," she shot back playfully, referring to their drunk aunt she was named after.

Joy sometimes felt she was marked from the day she was born, but she knew better. Everyone had their demons. Even their drunk ass Aunt Elaine. Besides, she had no time to feel sorry for herself and definitely no time to compete with what she knew didn't need to be compared.

They were sisters. Their love would always supersede a checklist of life's accomplishments, no matter what people thought. That wasn't so true, however, when it came to their sister, Mercy. They still loved her dearly, but Mercy was Pastor's little "do girl" who seemed to look down on the both of them, especially Joy who'd chosen not to go into ministry on any level.

"You know I hate that middle name, right?" she said. Still, they all loved their Aunt Elaine, especially around holidays. In fact, everyone loved a drunk relative then as long as she didn't sip and spill their tea.

"I know." Faith smiled.

"I do wonder though if that hoe's still drinking," Joy replied, tilting her head to the side. "We should call her," she suggested with a mischievous grin.

"You're so going to hell. Leave Auntie Elaine alone," Faith told her, rolling over and raining kisses all over her face.

"Shoot, Faith! Move," she fussed, playfully pushing her away. "I don't know where your mouth and hands have been."

"Nowhere if *Bossip* and *TMZ* had to tell it since my husband is giving away what's supposedly mine," she replied, winded as she flopped back on the bed. "And thanks for not telling anyone where I am. I promise to be gone in a few more days. Checking some things out. Oh, and I fired my publicist. That tramp still hasn't made a statement, and I don't want her to. It is what it is," she said as she prepared her exodus from Jonestown.

"Told you to hire me, but hey," Joy said, still feeling slighted behind it. She knew if anyone would have had her sister's back in that world, it would have been her.

"Un uh. So you and Rell could stay missing? I think not," she replied, referring to Joy's ex and Razz's best friend.

"On that note," Joy spat with an attitude, sitting up. "You can leave today. Don't nobody want to speak on Rellon's ugly ass."

"Oh, he's ugly now?" Faith laughed. "Well, I'll be sure to tell him you said that," she said, reaching for her cell when Joy tackled her. "Joy! Get off of me!"

"Faith, please don't," Joy begged with bucked eyes.

"Why, because you're being a whole whore out in these streets? I'm telling you, Joy, holding a grudge is bad for your heart, sissy."

"Says the girl playing in her vag about a man she wouldn't

dare share she was thinking about him to him," Joy shot back, sticking her tongue out at Faith.

"Yeah, well I guess we're both pretty screwed up," Faith confessed, taking Joy by the hand as they lay back and stared up at the ceiling.

"Yup, Pastor messed us up, sissy. He really did," she added as they cuddled up like they did when they were kids.

"I was thinking about heading to Mason, but I don't know," she said, shrugging her shoulders.

"Mason, you say?" Joy repeated, a huge smile plastered on her face. It was the kind of smile that spoke more than what was said that Faith seemed to have missed.

"Yeah. It's small, quiet, no one there will know me… I hope," she said, dragging her fingers through her hair. "Which reminds me, I need to cut and color this or something. What do you think?"

"I already told you, Faith. *Think* and live for yourself. I wouldn't cut my shit if it were long and healthy like yours, but I get it. Sometimes you have to cut ties to what you know to create new ones. Just leave your credit card. A bitch's refrigerator looking real crackhead-ish," she told her, causing them both to release a hearty laugh.

"Ugh, I hate you, Joy Elaine," she said, embracing her sister even tighter.

"I love you more, Faith Caroline. I really do."

Chapter One

Eight Years Earlier

"I can take these out to him," Faith told her mother, grabbing a few trash bags. Even though their father could afford a professional lawn service, Denver was all in now. What initially started out as a punishment, was now a gift. Over the past two years, Denver had come to not only enjoy attending to their lawn but found peace in it. Peace was a commodity he'd rarely called his own, but when he looked at Faith, that was all he felt—peace.

"Don't forget that glass of lemonade," her mother said excitedly. "You know Denver loves my lemonade," she bragged, smiling.

"Un huh, Mama," she replied with a smirk-like smile.

If asked, that infamous lemonade was what snagged their father and the men with wandering eyes each time First Lady

Valerie Valentine showed up. No one really knew what it all contained, which made it that much more intriguing as they all attempted to guess over the years. Her mother, however, would never confirm nor deny.

"And Faith likes giving him what he likes, too," her sister Mercy whispered to Joy. Faith's mocha colored skin flushed as she sucked her teeth. No one except her sisters knew she had a thing for Denver, and if she could keep it that way, she would. Besides, guys rarely approached the Valentine sisters. They weren't a mega church just yet, but her father had done a wonderful job giving the church in Jonestown some nationwide visibility, especially after it had been passed down two generations on to him.

"What?" their mother asked, confused, looking over her shoulder.

"Nothing, Mama," Mercy replied while Joy snickered, adding fuel to the fire.

Faith was pissed, clutching the kitchen towel as her nerves began to unravel. She looked forward to watching him mow the lawn. She would easily get lost as she sat perched in her bedroom window, gazing at him like the smitten teenage girl that she was. Every now and again, he'd catch her watching. Instead of making her feel embarrassed, he'd cast a wink her way, causing her to blush. So her mother sending her out there meant she didn't have to steal a glance. She could watch him in all of his sweat and glory immediately in his presence.

Being preacher's kids came with its own challenges, but the Valentine girls had done a great job covering for themselves, especially Mercy who hung around the church while Faith practiced for Sunday morning praise and worship on the piano. That secretly gave her extra time to grin in the boys' faces at church too afraid to speak to her around their parents.

That included Knight, one of Denver's closest friends at church. He was quiet yet alluring as he usually sat off in the cut alone yet didn't go unnoticed. His dark chocolate skin and menacing stare were a treat to see as Mercy got a sweet tooth prancing around him. Still, he wouldn't bite.

"Well, go on now. The boy's sweating, child. I already feel bad Theo barely pays the boy, even though he says he doesn't want to be paid," her mother said, nudging her on as she grabbed mittens out of the kitchen drawer. Faith grabbed the glass, feeling the lemonade spill due to her shaking hands. She could barely focus as she watched his firm abs as he lifted his shirt, wiping his face.

He's beautiful, she thought to herself as he then grabbed the weed eater. When he roughly yanked on the starter chord and brought it to life, Faith's breath hitched, causing the lemonade to spill even more.

"Dang it," she grumbled as she made her way out to the wooden table in their backyard to place it down along with the garbage bags.

As Denver swiped the weed eater back and forth against the edge of the lawn with ease, Faith took a seat so she could indulge in his every movement. From the way he twitched his jaw to the way he stretched his back, she was enamored. There was nothing no one could say to make her think otherwise about the boy many whispered she should stay away from.

Raised by his grandmother, Denver had it rough, but one thing he and his younger sister, Brianna, had was love, a love Faith could see in his eyes whenever theirs connected. She never believed in love at first sight, but if it existed, it started with her and Denver.

Faith became so consumed with the peanut butter colored boy with the devilish, infectious smile and lips she wanted to feel on hers, she'd ignored the irritated visitor in the form of a wasp until it made its presence known.

"Argh!" she screamed, swatting at her leg as the wasp buzzed around. "It stung me!" she cried out. In an instant though, he was no more when Denver caught it with one hand that formed into a tight fist, killing it.

He cursed lowly, watching a few others buzz around the sunflowers, sunflowers he'd planted just months earlier because he knew they were her favorite.

"It-it stung me," she repeated, her chest heaving up and down with misty eyes. When he saw them, he became angry. Dropping the weed eater, he shook the wasp out of his hand.

"I know, Faith. Fucking wasp," he whispered as he leaned down to stare at the reddish bruised skin on her leg. Her eyes fluttered, matching the flutter she felt in her belly when he swooped her up and carried her inside.

Her already racing heart doubled in speed feeling the warmth and wetness of his skin, the strength of his arms. But what drew her in even more was the smell of the sun coupled with cologne. She didn't know much about cologne, but whatever he wore was her favorite scent. Yes, his unique smell alone, she'd coined "the Denver", a wood-scented fragrance that easily could send her to the moon each time she inhaled it.

At sixteen, Denver moved like a grown man, spoke like one too. It excited Faith, made her feel alive since he was the only boy that dared to even speak to her. Unlike other boys his age, Denver gave no fucks about who her father was or knowing she was untouched. In fact, he wanted his woman untouched and tucked away, reserved just for him.

"I need warm water and baking soda," he demanded as her mother and sisters looked at them both confused as they headed their way. "Now," he demanded, then apologized. He was frustrated as he felt her body trembling against his. "It's going to be okay, Faith," he assured her with dark, piercing eyes, eyes that studied her trembling lips. Lips he wanted to suck, lick, and pull on as he fought hard to stay focused, closing his eyes as he turned his head.

It wasn't for long though; he felt the graze of her fingers against the back of his neck. When she did, he was in sensory overload, studying her heart-shaped lips and chinky, brown cedar eyes that made him misstep. He quickly steadied himself as she held on tighter, her face now in the crook of his neck.

"Shit, sorry," he told her, trying to stay focused until he could get her inside. When his eyes traveled back down to her mouth, he silently begged her to tuck in her lips. If she didn't, he feared he wouldn't be able to contain himself, and truthfully, he didn't want to. It was crazy how while speechless, Faith could get Denver to do anything she wanted or needed him to do.

"I'm in fucking trouble," he said just above a whisper to himself as they approached the door. "It's okay," he told her as she whimpered. She agreed, smiling while a hiccup escaped her mouth.

"Sorry," she said, covering her mouth.

"Never be sorry for being yourself which is sweet. Wasp couldn't help itself," he said and smile as he stepped inside and lowered her into a chair her mother had pulled out and waiting.

"Oh my God. What happened?" her mother asked when she saw the bruise in tears.

"A freaking wasp sting. I need an ice pack too, please," he replied, as he dropped to his knees. Thank God Faith was wearing a sundress to cover her legs, flowing just below her knees. He groaned, watching her rapidly blinking eyes when her mother handed her a napkin.

"Oh, honey, I feel awful," she said, watching Faith sniffle before she blew her nose. "Mercy, don't stand around. Get some ice and put it in a bag," she said while Joy worked on getting the baking soda and water.

"How bad is it?' she asked Denver as he examined her otherwise flawless skin short of the red area where the wasp had stung her. She was perfect in every way as his eyes traveled up her legs and torso before landing on her face. She was being a little fighter, pushing out a smile, he assumed not to disappoint him. He felt responsible though, wishing he'd never planted those flowers. It didn't help she smelled like she'd been dipped in a pot of honey too, a smell that would forever be embedded in his brain and in his heart. Probably like the wasp that couldn't wait to taste her too.

"Not too bad," he said, feeling his nature swell as he cleared his throat. "I need to get rid of those flowers," he announced roughly under his breath. "Where's the ice, Mercy? Joy, that baking soda and water coming any time soon?" he barked, frustrated.

"Dear God," her mother whispered, watching him attend to her child in such a loving manner. She fought back tears watching him softly blow on her leg, causing Faith's breath to hitch once more as an adrenaline rush coursed throughout her body.

Her mother knew that look and that reaction too, speechless when Mercy and Joy appeared.

"Mama, here's the ice," Mercy whispered, in tears herself while Joy stood by blinking back her own tears.

"Thank you, dear. Need us to do anything else?" her mother asked Denver.

"Naw," he said. "Hold that ice, Mercy," he instructed her, before whipping up a paste concoction of baking soda and warm water in the cup. Once he was satisfied with the outcome, he gently applied it to her leg with his fingers before rubbing it in slowly. Each time she winced from his touch, he fought hard not to groan.

"The ice is for swelling. I can see a little swelling now, but let me work this in just a little. That's cool with you?" asked her, and Faith nodded.

Her mother and her sisters stood by in awe, but no longer because of the wasp bite. It was because of the budding romance that unfolded right before their eyes. He studied every inch of her leg, calf included, lifting it gently as his jaw twitched. He held back words that begged to be released, words ranging from anger since she was in pain to adoration because he loved her. Loved her just for being her, while trusting him at the same time. He wanted Faith, and not just her body. He wanted everything, including the air she breathed in that moment when she whispered his name.

"Yes, Faith?" he answered lowly, gently pressing the bag of ice against her leg he held. He was afraid to look up. He knew if he did, it would be clear that this was a boy willing to fight the world for her, even a gang of wasps outside doing what wasps do—stinging people who got in their way.

"I'm sorry I got stung."

"Don't be sorry, girl. Stop tripping." He laughed, casting a quick glance at her. "I told you. Just keep being you," he reminded her. "I like the you that you are," he added, a bit bold right in front of her mother as her sisters giggled. She blushed, chewing on her bottom lip as her heart leaped for joy. It was then she knew that he liked her too, maybe even loved her. Not just playing with her whenever he winked when she sat in her window.

"Well, I guess this time it wasn't my lemonade that got the boy," her mother said to herself, chuckling as she swiped the tears that threatened to fall.

A year later, Denver's presence in the Valentines' home increased, and it was more than him attending to their lawn. He was First Lady Val's unofficial son who'd somehow found things around their home that needed fixing. Things their father agreed to get to but never did. In fact, Faith would break things like the spoke on her bicycle tires just for Denver to figure out a way to fix it, buying them more time just to be around each other. A blind man could see the two had fallen for each other, and they hadn't done more than hold hands.

"Faith?" Mother Daniels said and smiled as she entered the sanctuary. "Make sure you play my favorite song today," she told her, swatting at her grandson. "And stop following this child around and find something to do."

"Grams, come on now," he said, grinning as he blushed. "I'm headed to Sunday School. Just took a shortcut," Denver semi-lied since he was headed out back behind the church. The truth was that he only attended Sunday School whenever Faith did, but she didn't on second Sundays. Second Sundays were the days she not only led the youth choir but also played the piano and sang the lead.

"Make sure you leave that five dollars in the plate, sir," his grandmother instructed him. It was just like him and Knight to find a way to double that before service, playing dice behind the church building.

"Yes, ma'am," he replied with a tight smile as Faith snickered. That five dollars was just as good in a dice game the second he was out the back door. Then if he won, he'd have a Slurpee and Lemonheads for her after church. Denver was always so thoughtful, so kind but only when it came to three women—Grams, Brianna and Faith, his Mouse. He called her that over time since she was petite and moved around fast like a little mouse.

"Faith, don't let my grandson distract you from being about the Lord's business, now," she warned her, smiling as the two stood there looking at each other all googly eyed.

"Yes, ma'am."

"Dang. Grams stay trying me," he whispered in Faith's ear. "Imagine that, me getting Mouse into trouble," he said, bumping her lightly on the shoulder.

"Stop calling me that," she whispered, as she watched him gaze down at her lovingly when they took off. Her heart skipped a beat when he did before her body slammed into the back of someone.

"Dang, girl," Razz snapped, issuing a menacing stare her way. "Are you blind, Preacher Girl?" His eyes shot in Denver's direction when he did whose jaws were twitching. "Watch where you're going," he warned her.

"And if she don't?" Denver countered with an evil grin on his face. "Trust me. You don't want these problems. Not when it comes to her," he added, leaning down and whispering in his ear. "That fuck up I accept behind the way I kick your ass will be worth it."

"Sad, all over some pussy you won't ever get. But then again…" he said, staring down at an angry Faith. Her dress was a bit sleeker, hugged her petite frame just a little more. Ass he didn't realize she had was more prominent, and her breasts weren't that small. "That so-called ass whooping might be worth it," he told him. Truth is he wasn't into church girls, but he was prepared to make an exception just to get under Denver's skin.

"Faith, is it?" he added, tucking in his lips.

"Don't address her," he warned him. He felt Faith's small hands around his forearm when they heard someone clearing their throat nearby. Faith's body immediately stiffened. When she tried to release his arm, Denver refused to let her as her father stepped in front of them.

"Boys, meet me after church in my office," Pastor Valentine said with a tight smile while looking his daughter's way. By then, Faith had managed to free herself as she smoothed her dress down. "Faith, don't you have to get ready for the service?"

"I am, Daddy. I was just headed to get my robe," she replied, followed by a nervous laugh.

"Then do that," he told her, motioning her along with his hand.

Once she took off, he looked at Razz and Denver, chuckling lowly as they engaged in a mean mug battle. While he loved Denver like a son, he knew Denver had his trouble dealing with figures of authority. With no father in sight, he didn't trust men easily and didn't care to be around them. While he knew being his pastor created a relationship that Denver didn't necessarily sign up for, being his daughter's boyfriend was not one he approved of.

As for Razz, he'd counseled him more times than he cared to admit. He was an angry hot head who often initiated more fights than he could finish. But if the boy had one thing he admired, it was his need to be seen and heard.

Still, both came from good families who had been

attending Piney Grove Ministries for years. Razz's grandmother, Mother Long, had been around just as long if not longer than Denver's grandmother. They were well respected and loved in the church, fighting daily to raise two rebellious young men.

"Raziel, I got a call from the school this week, and you need community service hours. In fact, you need them as a condition to graduate," he stressed, rolling back and forth on the ball of his feet. "I wonder where you've been spending your free time, because it's not here at the church."

Denver chuckled, wondering why Razz tried to be something he wasn't. He knew where Razz spent his free time. That was in the streets pretending to be a hustler. It was all to prove a point to his Uncle Solo his grandmother had long ago cut ties with.

"I don't know anything about no community service hours," he lied, his face contorted even more as he watched Denver smile at his expense. "Why the school calling you anyway?"

"Maybe because this is your last opportunity to be a productive citizen in Jonestown. Now look, son," he said, grabbing him on the shoulder. "I take great interest in all of my boys. Denver, you too," he added, looking his way. "And I'd rather keep it like that so I can be of help. God has a plan for all of us. It's up to us where we fall in that plan," he told him. "Denver, add Deacon Monroe's yard after mines next Saturday since you have so much energy to expend."

"Pastor Theo?" he challenged, sucking his teeth when he felt a pop to the back of his head. "Grams, come on now."

"What did the pastor say?" This time it was Razz's turn to laugh.

"Yes, ma'am," was all he said while his eyes remained

trained on Razz. "Adding Deacon Monroe's yard next Saturday. Yo, Pastor Theo? I still need to see you after church?"

"No, son," he said. "But that doesn't mean this is over," he said as a soft melody was heard in the background.

Instantly, Denver's attention shifted as Faith sat on the piano gracefully playing the song his grandmother had requested. She was his angel on earth, his heartbeat in human form. He was spellbound like always in her presence. The look on his face wasn't missed either when Pastor Valentine patted him on the back.

"Let's go, son," he said, chuckling. "I can add a few more yards before you get yourself into trouble. Razz, I still need to see you though."

"Yes, sir," he said, his eyes fixed on Faith. She played effortlessly with closed eyes as the spirit of God filled the atmosphere.

It was like that for her, too. Whenever she placed her fingers on the piano keys, Faith was in another place and time while transporting others along with her. She was a gift to the body of Christ. To Denver too, who shot Razz a look of death when that same spellbound look graced his face as if he were in love too.

Chapter Two

It was Sunday. Sundays were always reserved for a huge, family dinner at the Valentines after Pastor preached two services. As his congregation began to grow, their need for a larger sanctuary became necessary. He'd spent months working with his chief financial officer who was his best friend, Deacon Monroe, and other ministerial staff, identifying ways to generate revenue to construct or purchase a larger building.

One idea was gaining the support of the community using music as the center. He knew he was taking a leap with this, but the church sat in a lower to middle class, black neighborhood. Pastor Valentine loved them dearly and the community he served. They were also a community that struggled with bringing money in, and sometimes more went out to meet their needs than what came in. Yet music always seemed to be something that could bring a large group of people together. Music and food, that is. Especially church folks. So he invited someone to dinner with hopes he'd solved his problem.

"Daddy, someone's at the door," Joy called out. Joy was

thirteen going on twenty-five. She was the sassy, vocal sister with rich chocolate skin and a head full of hair. Her big, brown eyes and bushy eyebrows made her request for almost anything undeniable by everyone, especially her mother.

"Valerie?" he said, calling to his wife. He didn't like the girls sashaying around the house when company came, not before Sunday dinner. His wife sighed, just about to pull out a fresh pan of her Mexican cheese cornbread. It was something she'd whipped up as an experiment.

Faith, being the eldest at seventeen, heard her and quickly stepped in, especially since they'd all been at church since seven that morning. She watched her mother rise up before sunrise to make sure their father had a waiting fresh pot of coffee. That and a full spread of breakfast by six o'clock so her family could be fed before heading out for church. The poor woman barely slept the night before since she started Sunday dinner on Saturday night.

"I have it, Daddy," Faith called out. Drying her hands off after washing up the dishes, she made sure she was presentable before she went to answer the door.

"Joy?" she said, looking down at her who was on her heels. She was thin as a rail, wearing a spaghetti strap dress with nothing on her arms. Joy already knew what Faith was referring to. She rolled her eyes before she spun around and stomped off. She loved playing dress up, consumed with how she looked. That, and she never missed a moment to be in the spotlight. While some thought it was cute, many had never met a thirteen-year-old that was into fashion and one who enjoyed making a statement like Joy.

"You already know Mama and Daddy don't play that," she grumbled to herself as she heard Joy slam her bedroom door before flipping her a birdy. "Grown behind."

Mercy was in her room doing what she usually did—coming out when sanctioned to come out or to take a peek at any new visitors. She was the shade of lightly creamed coffee, slim figure with an athletic type of body from being in the dance ministry.

"Coming," Faith called out before looking down at herself to tug on her dress. It was long but even she had to admit she was filling out as it rested just above her knees.

At home, they were allowed to dress more casually, but for dinner, she still tried to wear a dress. She'd slipped on a burnt orange sundress that complemented her mocha complexion. With her thickly waved hair swooped up, she finished her look off with gold earrings and gold sandals, her favorite pair.

When Faith opened the door and saw who stood before her, shock soon morphed into a scowl accompanied by a deep-rooted anger. It was Razz, cockily standing there, unveiling her from head to toe. She'd been avoiding him since the Sunday before, and successfully too, only for him to show up at her home as if he were happy to see her.

"So, Preacher Girl, that's how you treat a guest?" he asked, taking notice of her small, firm hips and beautifully manicured toes. What Denver saw that Sunday back then was accurate as his interest soon shifted into more of a personal one as he smiled, nodding his head at the view before him. She was mesmerizing, causing his lips to curl in each corner as she frowned. A few tresses that dangled in her face, cascading down her shoulders. Shoulders she knew she should have covered before she opened the door as he took notice.

"Uh, what are you doing here?" she probed under her breath, tightly gripping the door handle.

"What do mean what am I doing here?"

"Faith, everything's okay?" her mother asked, coming

behind her when she saw her standing there longer than expected. "Oh, Raziel. It's you."

"Razz, ma'am. Just call me Razz," he told her, as she motioned for Faith to step back and let him in. "Good afternoon, Miss Valerie, and thank you for having me."

Strangely, although she'd never admit it, she had no clue Raziel was coming. Still, she greeted him with a smile. She figured the invite either slipped her mind or it was her husband doing Mother Long a favor, having yet another fatherly talk with her troubled grandson. Either way, there was plenty of food since she'd always made enough for Denver if he stopped by. She'd even send him home with a plate or two with a jar of her lemonade.

"Oh, you are more than welcome. Dinner's almost ready. Faith, get Razz some fresh lemonade and sit with him in the family room until dinner's ready," she said, closing the door before she swiftly took off to check on her cornbread.

She'd worked too hard on this new recipe and too tired to whip up something else in its place if it burned. Her mother missed the roll of Faith's eyes as he chuckled, leaving the two of them alone. Faith wasn't excited about serving him anything, especially her mother's lemonade. It wasn't because she believed that it was magical like the myth that surrounded it. His existence alone just annoyed her.

"Can't stand him," she groaned, as he walked in further, looking around. He'd never visited their home, often curious about how they lived, and instantly, he was impressed. It wasn't too fancy when thinking of infamous black families since they were high up there in Jonestown.

Faith Caroline stared at him suspiciously, unsure as to when her father and Razz had become close. She just prayed this was the first and *only* time she'd have to stomach him through a meal.

"Can y'all tell me why Razz is here?" she asked Mercy who came out on cue and found her way to the kitchen as Faith poured his drink.

"I don't know why, but he is so fine," Mercy whispered as she watched their father waved him over to the patio door. "The guest list are definitely more to my liking."

Groaning, Faith Caroline nudged Mercy when suddenly, Joy popped in there and squealed as soon as she saw him out back.

"Joy, please. He's a menace. Nothing to get excited about unless you're fascinated with becoming a prison wife in your future," Faith said nastily.

"Faith, girl. Stop judging," she said, with a little skip until she stood next to them.

"Shoot, I wonder what Daddy is up to myself now that you say it," Mercy added, peeking out the window as they walked out of their sight. Though close to sixteen, she'd been forbidden to date while Faith had somewhat been given permission. It was her choice that didn't sit well with her father while Mercy hid her boy craziness and, like Joy, Razz definitely piqued her interest.

"Now that I think about," Faith mumbled, looking out the window too. "Probably writing a letter to his probation officer. Never know with Daddy," she concluded quite disgruntled as she head out back to give him his lemonade.

"Wait," Mercy said, grabbing her arm.

"Girl, what?" she snapped as her two sisters barricaded her in the kitchen full of curiosity. By then, their mother was setting the table with their best china.

"Let's just ask," Mercy said, answering her own curiosity. "I bet he has a girlfriend… a few of them," she continued.

"That would mean he has *girlfriends* as in plural. See, Joy, why he's nothing to get excited about?"

"That's even more exciting," Joy replied, dropping a few ice cubes in the chilled glasses prepared for them to drink out of. If nothing else, their mother was southern fancy when it came to just about everything.

"God, help me," Faith mumbled, pouring lemonade into a glass as she swatted a fly that danced in her face. "As for girlfriends, I'm sure he's not interested in church girls. So chill."

"He doesn't have to. I'm just admiring from afar. Besides, Knight's my man," Mercy said, giggling. The most they'd done was talk in Sunday School or after church, but Knight wasn't pushing it. Not when Mercy was two years younger. Besides, he had bigger fish to fry, like being in foster care and hustling to provide for two siblings which was how he and Denver had met.

"And Razz will be mine," Joy whispered as Mercy snickered.

"Don't encourage that, Mercy. Please don't."

"Don't be like that, Faith. Everyone can't be like your precious Denver."

"What about me?" they all heard Denver ask as he snuck up on them. As soon as he did, she felt warm coupled with a flutter in her stomach. She fought hard to keep the smile she knew was trying to emerge at bay. A smile that only appeared in his presence or when she thought of him. It was that same goofy one his grandmother caught and her mother worried about. One that made her look slow and spaced out and that was only reserved for him.

"Why am I not surprised? The goofy look," Mercy whispered as Faith shushed her.

"What's up with ya'll? Mouse?" he said, greeting her with a smile as he wrapped his lanky arm around her neck. He was sweaty too, sweaty and smelled like freshly cut lawn coupled with his woody infamous scent. "Sorry, I'm late. I had Deacon Monroe's yard to knock out. Couldn't get to it yesterday."

"So you came without a shower?" Joy sassed as her top lip touched her nose.

"Hush up, fast behind girl," Faith told her. "The towels are down the hall. You have time to wash up in the guest bedroom… I mean, if you want to," she told him dreamily, but she'd rather he not. She could inhale that scent for hours. Heck, days if Denver was the carrier of it.

"Thanks, Mouse," he whispered against her ear. "Always looking out for me. Who's the lemonade for?" he asked, grinning as his mouth began to salivate.

"Mama asked Faith to take it to our guest," Mercy replied, as she looked over her shoulder toward the patio. She knew the boys weren't friends, eager to see how this would pan out.

"Well, until they show up, I guess that means this is a glass for me," he said, grinning. He then slowly lifted the glass, tossing his head back as he began to drink.

As he did, Faith practically fainted as she watched his Adam's apple bob up and down as he gulped slowly. She was used to the flutter that danced about in her stomach, but what she felt then wasn't a flutter. At least not when it appeared between her legs as she squirmed to make it stop.

"Sugar cane with a hint of mint," he whispered even softer to her, causing goosebumps to clothe her mocha-colored skin before he finished it off. "I'm right, huh?" he challenged her before he pinched her cheek.

"No one knows mama's lemonade recipe," Faith replied sassily as she recovered, taking the glass from him.

"I'll keep trying though. Who knows? Maybe one day I'll figure it out," he said as he took in the dress she was wearing. It was a bit shorter than he'd liked and he wasn't feeling her bare shoulders at all as he stared her suspiciously. He knew how hard it was for him to maintain his composure around her himself sometimes, but he'd hate to have to check their guest when he asked, "You mind telling me why the hell is Razz over here? The fuck we need his non-hustling ass around?"

"How would I know?" she spat in disbelief, hearing the venom in his voice. She knew they weren't necessarily friends, but the emotions he'd just conveyed as he spoke seemed to run deeper than hate.

"It's all good," he released as his smile reappeared, tugging on her chin. "As long as he knows you're my Mouse."

"I know that's right," Joy chimed in, as Faith shot a disapproving look her way.

"Oh, God. This is going to get good," Mercy said as soon as their mother called out to them, wondering what was taking them so long.

"Your daddy's a trip for real," he told her after Mercy and Joy were gone. "Just know for you, shit's real. I won't ever play when it comes to my Mouse and he's a fuck boy. Your daddy better watch him because I sure the fuck will," he told her, quickly pecking her lips. It was their first kiss and when he did, she blinked a few times as he slowly took a step back and grinned. "Shit's sweet. That's *my* sweet Mouse. Now come on, girl. Let's go."

Chapter Three

"How much this time, Rock?" Solo asked Denver after he'd stopped by just before he woke up. To the church, he was Denver, but into the streets where he hustled, he was Rock. It signified how hard he brought it when it came to how he got his money.

Solo had been watching Denver for a few years, impressed with how focused he was and how silently he moved. If one looked at him, you'd see a menacing, quiet church boy in a basic white tee shirt, jeans, and white Jordans with no jewelry in sight.

Unlike others, Denver's money went to pay his grandmother's bills and to provide for his sister, not in his mouth or around his neck and wrists. And if he copped a piece of jewelry, it was for one girl and one girl only—his Mouse. Jewelry she often hid but loved with all of her heart.

Solo initially recruited him to piss his nephew Razz off, but ever since he did, his move proved to be quite fruitful as Denver brought in more than others twice his age. He refused to work for anyone, and up until now, he hadn't. Yet Solo knew eventually, the negotiating for more product at a lower price would begin. Denver, along with Knight, were wise well beyond their years, and their hustle was proof of it.

"Double from the last time," Denver told him. His back was to the side of the door that was slightly ajar as he looked outside. He had a few hours to get the money up his grandmother needed to pay last month's rent, but he knew he had to strike while the iron was hot. It was the first of the month, and the fiends were ready to exchange food stamps for crack rocks, and he had to have it.

"And that Holy Hell shit, too. None of that weak ass gas your nephew slid me the last time you weren't here," he snarled, looking around for Razz. "Should bust his ass," he growled lowly. He had no fucking clue what was in it, but the product Solo had been giving him as of late moved faster than hell and sent the fiends to the moon just like its name.

He and Knight lived double lives out of necessity, never out of greed. As long as he reminded himself that this was temporary, he stayed focused with an endgame in mind—that was working for himself, no matter how much Solo praised him. He wanted not only his own lawn service company but a few other avenues of revenue he and Knight were still brainstorming.

"Word?" Solo said, shaking his head as he sat up. He then motioned for him to close the door so they could handle business. "Like that? Neph must have done that shit by accident," he said, smiling with hopes of smoothing things over.

"Yeah, like that with his bitch ass," he replied, swiping the end of his nose as he frowned. He was tapping his pocket too as his head swiveled around canvassing the room. Denver had no clue why Solo laid where he played, but he had no intentions of finding out while Tressa, his Holy Hell tester, waved at him. She was on the sofa naked as the day she was born.

"I see you, youngin, and I know you're strapped, but only because I let you," he told him, laughing as he gave one of his men the nod to go and get Denver his product. "You just make sure Mother Daniels don't know shit," he added since their grandmothers were close friends.

"My grams not even checking for me and tell his ass to hurry up. I got to get home. I got to make moves before youth bible study tonight."

"Yeah, yeah. Relax, youngin. I remember those days. The bitches stayed offering me the pussy. I'm sure not much has changed."

"I wouldn't know," he said with a shrug of his shoulders. Not when all he saw was Faith. "Fuck them hoes," he replied while Solo nodded, leaning back as Tressa crawled over to him ready for the next round which including sucking his dick.

"Here you go, Unc," Razz said. He glared at Denver who was close to unleashing the beast in his hip.

"That Holy Hell shit?" Solo asked Razz, eyeing Denver's hand that was twitching.

"Yeah, this it," Razz said, smiling as he winked his eye quickly. It didn't go unnoticed either as Denver sucked his teeth.

"This lil' bitch. He wanna be me so hard," he said to himself. Everyone knew he only had the clout he did because of Solo, but even that came with him name dropping every chance he got. That and the rumor of him bring a snitch. While unconfirmed, the rumor alone made him suspect.

"What's up, Rock? Pastor know you're out here doing the devil's work? Thought you was his lawn boy."

"Your mama knows you're selling the same shit that got

her spaced out and fucked up?" Denver shot back, wondering how someone whose mother was an addict could sell drugs then judge others.

"My mother's on pills, bitch nigga," he disputed as Solo stood back watching and grinning. "Unc, you hear this? Like his own mama the mother of the year. All at Pastor's house faking and shit," he added.

"Whatever makes your fuck ass sleep good at night. My mom's business and location are none of your concern. You just make sure you don't end up like your moms, you pussy. Besides, ain't you a rapper or singer? Sounds like it's you that's the one faking," he shot back, dropping the duffle bag of money he'd owed Solo on the table in front of them.

"Yeah, a nigga got talent besides slinging dope. Oh, and getting hoes," he slid in, watching Denver fume. He was close to saying damn that product after Razz shot a subtle slug his way referring to Faith.

It was no secret he'd been eyeing her as of late, being extra friendly, especially once her hips and ass continued to grow in size to go with a smile that made Razz lose all common sense. It had been six months since that day he stopped by, and while he thought of her every day, Faith stayed dodging him yet was always seen smiling in Denver's face.

"Pfft, this shit don't take talent, hoe nigga. It takes heart. Heart your bitch ass don't have and will never have. Trust me, this shit here has an expiration date," he said, as Solo silently ended their feud as he picked up the duffle bag.

"You're not going to count that?" Razz probed, a scowl decorating his face.

"Rock's always on point. If I have to count it, I'd have to kill him," Solo said coolly, grinning as reached over and slapped hands with Denver.

"Not if I have to kill you first," he shot back through gritted teeth.

"Bitch, you threatening him?" Razz barked, walking toward him when Solo halted him with one hand to the chest.

"Calm down, neph," he told him, respecting Denver who hadn't flinched once. "Rock and I are cool. If he dropped it, the money's there. Ain't that right, Rock?"

"Whatever. Catch you at church, *Rock*," he replied, his voice laced with sarcasm as Denver chuckled before he eased out quietly. He was done tongue wrestling with Razz since he had to stop by the pawn shop to get the television his grandmother had pawned before church. He was living two lives with ease, working overtime until he could put this life behind him. The last thing he was about to do was to let Razz get in the way.

"Glad when this shit is over," Denver grumbled as he and Knight swiftly walked on the other side of town where the pawn shop was.

"I'm with you, D. Shit's getting crazy. The hell you was in there so long for?" he asked him, tucking his Glock behind his back.

"Why else? Hoe ass Razz. Stay worrying about Faith," he huffed while Knight laughed.

"Faith ain't even gave up the pussy, yet you ready to die for her. D, Solo not letting you take his nephew out. Remember, chess, not checkers," he told him, tapping the side of his temple.

The next week, Solo's place was raided, and before the police could arrest him, he'd died of a heart attack. Not many knew the location of where he'd kept most of his stash, but everyone who did had been arrested. Yet the only one that was released and his charges were dropped was Razz.

Word on the streets was it being related to a technicality, but Denver knew better. Razz had gotten in the bed with someone, making him a rat. Pastor Valentine worked with the District Attorney's office, testifying on behalf of Denver and Knight's character. While they cut Knight some slack since he wasn't caught with product, only affiliated with Denver, his friend wasn't so lucky. He had product and a gun, yielding him not only an arrest but a conviction.

"Denver Malachi Daniels, you've been sentenced to seven years in the Petersburg Correctional Facility. And trust me when I say I went light. I don't want to see you here ever again, Mr. Daniels. Use this time to reflect on rehabilitation so when you're released, maybe, just maybe you'll have a testimony to share. One that can detour other young, black men," the judge said as Razz sat back and smiled.

The room exploded with objections from the community. Everyone loved Mother Daniels, a pillar in her own right, but they loved Denver even more. He had nineteen church members speak on his behalf, his Sunday School teacher included, but even that wasn't enough.

He cast a glance at Faith who stood nearby, trembling as tears trickled down her cheek. She was a tight ball of emotions that spiraled out of her control as her father pulled her in, shielding her from the cameras. Mostly because this wasn't a good look for him, his daughter, or his church. That and he was already in dire straits financially. Being caught up in Denver's poor choices was bad publicity he wanted no parts of once he didn't get off.

"Let's get out of here, sweetheart," he whispered as she held on to him, crying.

"I'll write you, Mouse, every day. You hear me? Every day," Denver called out, watching them both slip out the door.

As soon as they did, he dropped his head as his heart fell in the pit of his stomach. That day was the day he began to die inside. The day she walked out of that courtroom and out on him. He had no desire to ever love again. Not when shit wasn't the same without Faith, his Mouse. She was the only reason he felt anything besides anger and hatred. The only reason, and now she was gone.

Chapter Four

"Faith," her father said, acknowledging her as she stepped into his office. After dinner, she and Denver would usually sit out back and talk where she shared her latest song she'd written. Now he was gone, she'd rush off to her room and cry. If not that, she, Joy, and Mercy would lay around and watch television until the other two grew bored, leaving her alone. This night, however, before she took off like she always did, her father had summoned her to his office.

"Hey, Daddy," she said before she saw they weren't alone. She rolled her eyes at Razz who was seated in front of her father's desk, smiling. He didn't attend dinner, so she figured he must have just arrived, slipping in sneakily. He was always around somewhere, lurking, and her father was of no help since he usually invited him.

"Please speak, Faith," he told her. She sucked her teeth when he did. He wasn't sure if this was an act to mask how she might really feel about Razz, but as of late, he'd had turned over a new leaf and was one of their most active members at church. That included singing in the choir.

"Hey," was all she said, pulling the chair she sat in far away from him before she sat down.

"What's up?" he said and nodded, soaking in her slender, yet shapely legs that were partially covered as she wore a denim overall skirt. Still, he allowed his imagination to see things he'd only prayed she'd let him see now that Denver was out of the picture.

"Daddy?" she said, ignoring him as she slowly crossed her arms.

"Fine, Faith. I guess I'll get straight down to business then. I wouldn't want to keep Denver waiting." He smiled. "Wait, I can't. He's locked up," he replied with an attitude, shaking his head. Every day, all day, he would hear Faith speak about Denver. It was Denver this and Denver that, then she'd run to the mailbox as she waited for mail to come that never did. She'd even gone as far as to convince herself there was a valid reason, a missed number in her address on the envelope or the mail placed in the wrong mailbox. And because he'd never lied to her before, she had no reason but to keep hoping and waiting no matter how long it had been.

"Are you trying to be funny, Daddy?" she asked, knowing he was as Razz smirked. "I didn't know you had a problem with Denver and I."

"Of course not, honey," he said, sighing. "I don't. I'm just saying there are other things you could be doing with your time until he finds the time to write. That's all I'm saying. I'm sure he's missing you just as much as you're missing him," he said, trying to appease her.

His patience with this love affair her mother had allowed

to develop right up under his nose still didn't sit well with him. His daughter was a Valentine, his eldest child, and the one with the most talent. He'd be damned if she wasted it waiting on some guy, even Denver, whom he'd grown to love despite how troubled he was. Still, he needed his daughter in his time of need and bad. The last thing he wanted to do was piss her off with only a few months before she graduated and went off to school.

"Shoot, the way I see it, all he has is time." Razz chuckled, reaching for a glass of her mother's lemonade.

I pray you drown drinking it, she thought to herself as she looked her father's way, counting to ten to calm down. It was something she'd often tell Denver to do every time they saw Razz. Now it was her own mantra to relax as she felt his eyes all over her.

"Raziel, that's enough," her father warned him. "Are you ready to be serious, or am I wasting my time here?"

"Hmph. Seems like wasted time and a glass of mama's lemonade," Faith mumbled.

"And that's more than enough from you, Faith Caroline,' he replied, pointing his finger her way. "I expect more from you."

"I'm surprised since he's your new pet or protégé. Pick one," she shot back as both, she and her father, stood up.

"My apologies, sir," Razz intervened, extending his hands their way as he motioned for them to relax. He wasn't trying to piss her off either, not when what her father was about to propose to her was a win win for him too. "Look, it's my fault," he admitted, sighing as her father slowly sat down, his eyes locked in on his daughter's who'd refused to move.

"How so when you're the guest?" her father posed.

"Because I'm really digging your daughter if I'm being honest. I try to find ways to speak to her on a level she deserves. I suppose it just come out wrong, I guess," he admitted, watching her fists ball up tightly through his peripheral vision. "It's true, Faith," he said, slowly looking her way. "I think you're beautiful. I can barely talk around you unless I'm saying something slick or stupid. No offense," he added quickly, looking at her father. "I'm just saying I'm sure it's not easy being around me. So, again, I apologize."

"Faith?" her father said, with a lifted brow.

"Ugh," she groaned. "Apology accepted… I guess," she said, taking her seat once again.

"Now that's out the way, let's move on as to why I have you both here, but before I do, Raziel, watch it. Faith's not dating."

"What?" she replied, her mouth open as if he was implying she and Denver were not an item. They were beyond that. They were in love.

"I know what I've allowed, but really, Faith. Clearly, you're not ready if your only option can't even court you. I love Denver. You know I do, but it's time you start focusing on *your* dreams. That may require you putting relationships on hold… even for Razz," he added, looking his way.

"I respect that, sir," he said while Faith sat teary-eyed, fuming on the inside. Denver was her everything, and in a matter of seconds, her father had dismissed his value to her as if everything meant nothing. Nothing at all.

"As I was saying, the summer youth jam explosion is coming up next month, and thankfully so. God knows the community needs something. With that being said, that still gives me time to go over what I've been planning. I wasn't sure how to pull this off, but then I heard you, Raziel, one day after bible study. You were rapping and singing," he said, grinning. "The kids were enjoying it, but not only them. A few of the adults, the tithe paying kind, which matters," he said, shooting a wink in his direction. "And I was impressed, very impressed."

Faith was familiar with Razz's free shows in and outside the church, eagerly finding ways to be the center of attention. Most times she ignored him. His rhymes and lyrics were a tad bit rougher than what she preferred, if language meant anything. Still, she could tell he definitely had a creative flow that many could appreciate.

"Not gospel though, right? I mean, I've never heard him reference God," she said, pursing her lips as she looked his way.

"What you saying, though? God only blesses it if it's about Him?"

"No," she shot back, sitting up. "Just making a point that what you do isn't gospel."

"Actually, it's not, but it had to be good enough for you to know that. Don't tell me that you've been studying me and my lyrics," he flirted, grinning as her father cleared his throat.

"Faith, be careful." He'd often told her gifts came without repentance, so that didn't mean because it wasn't about God that it wasn't a gift.

"Sorry, Daddy."

"It's fine, sweetheart. I just need you to keep an open mind. But I've been praying, and just when I thought God wasn't listening, I heard Raziel, you know, doing his thing. I even ran the idea about him participating by Brother Taron and a few deacons."

"Brother Taron?" she repeated as her father referenced the minister of music. "Why him and without me?"

"Well, this year he came to me with a few ideas about the summer jam youth explosion, and I think it's going to be something special if we add something the youth wouldn't expect."

"I help Brother Taron every year with that. That's where I keep him in touch with what the youth like," she argued, shooting daggers Razz's way.

"And you still will. This year it will be you *and Raziel*," he clarified.

"Razz, sir. Just call me Razz."

"Well, you and Razz. Now, before you jump to conclusions and say no because of what you think you know, I want you to listen to him. Hear him out and listen to this," he said, pressing play before a light beat could be heard that caused Razz to close his eyes.

An occasional "yeah" and "uh" was heard before he eased into the first verse. Once he did, he spoke out as if he were performing to an arena of thousands, speaking on the goodness of the Lord. Faith even caught herself bobbing her head a little, as she soaked up the lyrics.

Her father caught that and smiled. He knew he had to find a way to speak her language, and it wasn't just by talking. It had to be through music. Once music came on, it was as if Faith had been ushered into another world.

"Well?" Razz asked her once it ended. Her father scooted up in his chair as he rested his forearms on his desk. "You're the chosen one, the one with a gifted creative flow for the Lord. I've heard you play and sing, and your lyrics hit hard," Razz told her, meaning it too.

Once his uncle died and his mother overdosed, Razz was in a dark place. Music was always his outlet, but now it was his lifeline to sanity. And once he beat that charge, he'd promised God he was living for him or would at least try. It was as if the opportunity to love and to live life differently had fallen in his lap.

"I think it's something we could work with," she admitted as her father's eyes lit up. Brother Taron had gained some nationwide notoriety with Piney Grove's mass choir but not enough to catch the younger population. Her father had also been trying to expand the church, and the church's building fund efforts weren't as fruitful as he needed them to be. That was no secret the harder he had the ushers pass that offering plate around.

"This is great news, baby girl," her father said, looking back and forth between the two of them. "Spring break's coming up. I really need you two to get together so we have enough time to make this happen and start rehearsing."

"Spring break?" she squawked, thinking of the plans she had to ride up to see Denver. She'd already sent in the paperwork to get on his visitation list. Her mother had signed it behind her father's back, but still, it was signed. She was going.

"Yes, is that a problem?"

"Actually, I have plans," she said, her eyes abandoning her father's under firmly dipped brows.

"Actually, you have to get permission first from me, and unless it's more important than the body of Christ, I'd say you're free. Very free," he said with finality as she rose up quickly.

"Mama already gave me permission," she challenged him, knowing that added fuel to the fire. He'd been trying to stay on her mother's good side as of late. That was no secret. "Plans have been made, Daddy," she said, her voice shaky.

He sighed, wondering how he could meet her halfway since halfway was better than nothing at all.

"What exactly are these plans, Faith?" he asked her through gritted teeth.

"I'm going to see Denver," she replied proudly, her chest sticking out.

"What? Denver?" Razz scoffed as he eyed her father evilly. "That's your spring break plans?"

"Raziel," her father cautioned him, holding his hand up. "Sweetheart, let's revisit this later," he released, frustrated with his wife. "I have a couple of other things I need to discuss with Raziel."

"Razz, sir," he corrected him.

"I prefer Raziel, to be honest. Less street-like," he told him, his voice firm which caused Razz to settle down and shut up. "I'll catch you tonight before bed," he then said to Faith.

"So he gets to stay?" she challenged him.

"I said we will speak later, sweetheart."

"Ugh," she fussed.

"Later, Faith Caroline," Razz said smugly, as she stomped off and slammed the door.

"If you're trying to impress her, try again," he whispered forcefully to Razz. "I have a lot to lose," he added. "This is what you said you wanted, right? We've been discussing this for months. I swear I did my part. Now it's time to do yours."

"I am, but it's not me. It's her being all mean."

"You like her, don't you?"

"Yeah, I do," Razz said, sighing as he thought of the lemon and honey scent that still lingered in the air after her departure.

He actually was enthralled with her, enjoyed the feistiness that came with her. He'd never even looked at any girl the way he looked at Faith. Now, she was the only girl he wanted, and it had nothing to do with Denver. Well, not anymore. He had a shot to do something and do it well, admittedly, not as good at hustling as he portrayed. But when it came to being a lyricist and singer, he'd rock the mic and the crowd in a half of a heartbeat, leaving them speechless.

"Then act like it," he said before he'd heard Faith yelped just outside his office when she and her mother collided.

"Mama?" she said, as she tried to catch her breath.

"Everything okay out here?" her father asked, quickly opening the door.

"Ye—yeah," Faith stammered when her eyes darted in her mother's direction, causing her to frown in confusion.

"I was coming to tell you that the movie you wanted to see with your sisters is about to come on," she said, wondering what had her daughter so spooked until she saw Razz. "Oh, Raziel is here. I see… again," she said, tilting her head as she smiled. She knew her husband had taken an interest in him, but his presence as of late was strange. "Staying for the movie?" she asked out of politeness.

"No, ma'am. And it's Razz. I prefer Razz," he said before he remembered what the pastor had said. "But Raziel works too." He laughed.

"I see," she said, as she rubbed Faith's shoulder. Her daughter was trembling. She wasn't sure what was going on, but she knew to address it later, especially when she caught the look on her husband's face. Things had been different since Denver's arrest, even before that. Whatever it was, had created a shift in their marriage.

"I have to get going, Pastor Valentine. Just let me know when you're ready."

"Oh, we're ready. Come by the church later this week on

Thursday for the praise team's rehearsal. That can be Piney Grove's first introduction of you and Faith performing together."

"That's what's up, sir," he told him before Faith exited madly down the hall.

Chapter Five

"This is really crazy," Mercy told her, holding on to the steering wheel tightly. "If he hasn't been responding to your letters, why would you just bust up there and show up?" she asked as Faith sat next to her, rocking back and forth. She was a nervous wreck. So nervous, she couldn't even drive.

She and Razz had long started performing together, and the summer youth jam explosion was a hit. It had done so well, they were being booked for other church events. While Faith enjoyed how God was moving, it didn't make her love or miss Denver any less.

"It's not crazy," Joy countered. "That's not like Denver. She should go up there and demand he gives her some act right."

"Coming from the one who spends her days giving people 'act right' with no results," Mercy shot back, sucking her teeth.

"Girl, you're just mad Knight stay avoiding you. He didn't even look your way when he got released," Joy replied, taunting her. "A list you would have never made in the first place."

"You think I care about being some prison wife like Faith does?" She laughed using Faith's words back on her, while Faith sat there speechless.

"Hoe, don't pretend I don't know how you begged Knight to reach out," Joy replied lowly, shaking her head when Faith lost it and screamed.

"Enough already! Just stop it! I can't take it anymore," she released, staring back and forth at the both of them. "I don't care what anyone thinks," she said, looking at Mercy before her eyes swung back to Joy. "And Joy," she said, before taking a deep breath. "That was mean. Knight has a lot going on too. He probably didn't reach out or respond to a lot of people. I just need my sissies, both of you, to be here for me. Denver is probably scared, scared I will turn my back on him, so he's trying to shut me out first. Trust me, I know him. Now just drive, Mercy. That's all I need you to do."

"Fine," she replied, rolling her eyes at Joy as she stared at her in the rearview mirror. "And I just don't want you hurt. Razz has been working hard with Daddy and you at the church, and now here we are running off to some prison. I want what's best for you, sissy. That's all, and Razz likes you… a lot," she said, taking her by one hand as she steered with the other.

"And Denver isn't? Damn, Mercy. Some kind of loyalty you have. We've known Denver for a long time. He's practically family. How can you turn your back on him so easily, especially when you know he and Faith are in love?" Joy asked her in disbelief. "That's like our brother."

"Apparently not Faith's," she replied, snickering, which caused them all to laugh.

"Right, that would be incest," Joy chimed in, pinching Faith's cheek as she leaned over from the back seat. "Sissy, Razz is cool, but I'm with you on this one. If Denver is where your heart is, ride this prison bid out."

"Oh God," Mercy grumbled.

Twenty minutes after sitting in the prison parking lot, Faith came out walking slowly with tears in her eyes. Her mouth agape yet nothing was said as she slid in quietly and closed the door.

"I knew it. I knew it," Mercy said, quickly opening up her door. "He had another girl up there, huh?" she seethed, looking at Faith like she was ready to kill him. "Let's go handle that hoe," she said, taking off one earring at a time.

The Valentine sisters were a force to be reckoned with if left to their own devices, but thankfully, they knew the Lord. It was their upbringing alone that kept them from being straight ratchet like many girls in Jonestown but now was not the time to be holy. Ratchet is what this occasion called for and they were ready.

"For once, I'm with Mercy. Let's do this shit," Joy announced, hopping out and slamming her door. She wasn't trying to remove earrings because out of the three of them, Joy had hands for days. Always did since the girls in church loved to come for her.

"No! No, that's not it," Faith quickly told them, as she looked around. Her eyes were misty as she fought back tears, wondering why he'd break her heart like that and so soon. "He-he removed me from the list and uh…" she said and paused, swallowing as she tried to catch her breath. "The prison banned me from coming back again."

For a year, Faith seemed to move around in a fog. She ate, slept, and went to church. She'd barely hung out with her sisters, and when she did, it was forced. She had no interest in anything, even abandoning her dreams of going off to school. She and Denver had sat around and applied to four colleges, two nearby so he could see her as often as she could, but the one she wanted to attend the most was Creekstown Conservatory School of Music. In fact, that was all she talked about, and Denver wanted nothing less for her. Now, it seemed he didn't even consider her feelings as life pushed him to move on without her.

"Banned, like you're some criminal. That bitch," Mercy spat. "I knew it, Faith. Him and his damn friend, Knight. Trust me, you're better off without him," she told her as they pulled her into a group hug. Even then, Faith still felt all alone. Alone and abandoned as the hole he'd pricked in her heart that had opened up wide for him, began to bleed out.

After a year of no contact except other inmates and officers, which was still limited in solitary confinement, Denver was released to general population. He'd graduated into adult life with nothing but hatred in his heart. He walked around as a man of few words, only speaking when necessary, and that was, most times, to his classification officer who demanded he accepted a detail to reduce his time.

Initially, he fought back, refusing to work for pennies. However, as the days grew longer and he saw others walking out those gates being released to their loved ones, he gave in and went to visit his counselor about a prison detail to reduce his time.

"How much time I can knock off?" he asked Ms. Cherry, whose breath smelled anything but sweet like fruit.

"Two months for every month, so a year becomes like six months," she replied, smacking as she chewed her gum. She grinned at him too, gazing at him with lust in her eyes as he sat back and shook his head.

"Not interested, bitch," he told her, sighing as he stood up. "The fuck I look like fucking with you when you look like an alligator and your breath smells like alligator ass, too. Fuck out of here," he told her, motioning for her to call the guards to come and get him.

"The hell you mean!" she spat when the door opened up quickly, catching her off guard. "War-Warden Ivory?" she stammered, slicking her thick plaits back which didn't help much. They'd seen better days eight months earlier, as she'd barely made ends meet to pay bills from her low-paying prison salary. What she had left went to gas to get back and forth to work, leaving little for self-care like a hairdo.

"Inmate Daniels, follow me," was all he said, turning around as he stood in the hallway. "Don't let me repeat myself," he said as Denver sucked his teeth.

"Wash that shit out with a gang of soap, Ms. Cherry. That gum flavor must be called ass almighty or something. Oh, and that name's a fucking fraud," he said, before the warden cuffed him and hauled him off.

He was plotting on getting a detail that could get him outside the prison. Faith had run out on him, leaving him stranded. He was so gone about that, he'd do anything to confront her and ring her fucking neck on sight about playing with his heart.

Especially when Denver's green finger for planting and maintaining a lawn were highly spoken of. So much so, surprisingly, the warden himself had sought him out to maintain his own lawn. While he did begrudgingly, in no time at all, his dick had somehow fell inside the warden's daughter's pussy.

For three years, they had their weekly meetup in the warden's shed. His daughter, Dashon, fed him anything he wanted—fried chicken wings, conch, fried fish, you name it, while he fed her what she seemed to want the most—his dick.

Denver wondered where her ferocious appetite came from and, more importantly, why him. She was free to fuck whoever she wanted, whenever she wanted, yet Dashon Ivory wanted Denver Malachi Daniels. She screamed his name out like church women belted hallelujah when the spirit hit them or when they pretended it did to get attention.

Over time, he'd decided to entertain her less and less. Especially after learning he'd soon be released. He had no time for relationships and definitely not with the warden's daughter. He even swapped out his outside detail to cleaning state buildings and hospitals. The idea came from none other than his good friend, Knight. With the help of his siblings, Knight was now the founder and CEO of Commodore Enterprise, a company that bought and sold financially struggling businesses.

"You ready?" Knight asked him, two months shy of his release date. While his visiting list was short, Knight visited faithfully once a month, which Denver initially wasn't feeling. He hated people seeing him caged in like an animal, eventually glad that Faith had moved on.

"Hell yeah, I'm ready." He laughed. "Brianna's definitely ready to dig in my pockets, but shit, what money I have?" he replied, simply talking out loud.

"Are you serious?" Knight replied, staring at him with furrowed brows. "As much as you looked out for me, King, and Queen. Hell, even putting me on. The fuck do you mean do you have money? As long as I have it, you have it. Stop playing, nigga, for real," he told him, waving him off. "Commodore Enterprises started with money I earned from working bullshit ass jobs in collections, but the hustle, the drive… shit, you taught me that," he told his friend, resting his elbows on the table as he looked around.

He noticed the female guards strolling by slowly and smiling. He found it to be comical too, since the only pussy he cared about he really didn't care about at all—Rayelle, a girl who worked for Commodore Enterprises that he'd met who had also been in foster care.

"Don't even ask," Denver told him. "I wouldn't stick dick to any of these bitches. I already told you how I was moving," he said, laughing. "And I had to cut her ass off. She still try hitting me up though, sending letters through other inmates that cut her daddy's yard."

"Still?"

"Hell yeah, and to be honest, I'm wrong as hell. Shorty was cool and all that, but why would I want to deal with the warden's daughter on some serious shit? Shorty's reckless too, not caring if her daddy's at home or not. And giving it up to an inmate," he said, realizing more and more he was just as reckless, if not more since his pending freedom was on the line.

"Shit, D. Maybe she didn't see you as an inmate."

"Or she likes fucking inmates," Denver shot back as they laughed, dapping each other up. "Baby girl don't play though. She's got a good head on her shoulders, but her daddy wouldn't have a clue. He keeps her sheltered, all in the church, working for the church and shit."

"Kind of reminds me of someone else."

"I wouldn't know," Denver replied, his chest tight from

Knight even referencing Faith. His head was fucked up as they approached four years of no contact. He'd written her everyday just like he promised, and they'd all come back. Then she removed her name from the list and he was done with it. He wanted to be upset, but he knew in his heart of hearts, Faith, his Mouse, deserved better. Definitely better than two visits a week for four hours in a room of inmates, eye fucking her.

"Yeah, I know," Knight said, clearing his throat. Sadly, he knew and Denver too. Faith wasn't checking for him. She was with Razz now and not only as in working with him, but they were now engaged. "Fuck her," he said, shrugging his shoulders.

"Aye, none of that," Denver shot back with a scowl on his face. He may not have been feeling her, but he'd be damned if he allowed anyone to speak on her inappropriately in his presence. "Chill. She did what she had to do."

"Had to or wanted to?" Knight posed, causing him to think.

"Both," he said, feeling anxious and angry at the same time as he hopped up, needing to take a walk. If he didn't, he'd end up knocking a C.O. or inmate out and probably getting his early release revoked. "Yo, I'm out. Got some shit to do in my room," he lied, dapping Knight up once more. "So, see you next month?"

"For sure, Rock," he said, smiling as Denver shook his head.

"There you go with that Rock shit, huh?"

"Hey, you're always Rock to me. This right here don't define me or you. Money either. Fuck what anyone thinks. Stay up, D. Love you, for real," he told him, pulling him in for a hug before Denver took off to his cell.

Chapter Six

Two Years Later

"This damn grass seems like it hasn't been cut in more than a year, maybe two," he said to himself, looking at the price Brianna had quoted the owner. As his business expanded, he had less time to go out and do an assessment, but this was one reason why he needed to make the time.

He had a schedule based on the size of the lot, which also contributed to how many hands he had on the job. He was now cursing to himself after sending two of his crew on to the next job with hopes of catching up to them in two to three hours.

"This is going to have to be a two-part, maybe three-part job," he said to himself, lightly tapping on the door as he took in the dead grass and patches of weed.

"Finished already?" the dark mocha-colored woman

answered as she swiped sweat off her forehead with the back of her hand. She'd been unpacking all weekend, stuck in her own little world. So much so, she'd forgotten all about the lawn until she received a reminder text.

"Uh, no," he said slowly as he emphasized the word 'no', not even looking up short of her thick ass thighs and well-manicured toes. "When's the last time the lawn's been cut?" he asked her, his head swiveling back toward the grass.

"Honestly, I don't know. I just purchased the property. What's the matter?" she asked, a slight attitude detected in her voice.

She'd been arguing with Roger, his parents, and hers all week, and she was sick of it. After two years of dating, she'd called it quits. All Roger wanted was a live-in maid and pussy with no marriage date in sight. After that, an ultimatum was met with a dare, and that dare was her accepting that he just wasn't ready.

He was a deacon at her mother's church, groomed to be her husband. She found out soon that deacons were freaks, just like any other man, as her father tried to tame his daughter's rebellious ways. She'd often been at odds with him, given all he did was work. She'd learned over time that acting out somehow was the only way to get his attention. Even as an adult.

"The matter is the grass is dead." *The fuck*, he thought, sucking his teeth. "Deader than dead. Do the sprinklers even work?" he asked, still looking down as he mumbled under his breath as he tugged on his fitted cap. He was thirsty and hungry too, pissing him off even more. Besides that, he wasn't feeling the attitude.

"Aren't you the lawn guy?" she sassed back, pursing her lips. When he pulled off his cap, her eyes lit up as his mouth dropped. His did too. He couldn't believe it was her, really her after the way he'd curved her.

He chuckled, canvassing her body that looked damn good years later. She'd lost a significant amount of weight, not that she was really that large, but that coupled with her short, texturized cut made her look like a totally different person.

"Damn, Dashon. What's going on, girl?" He laughed, feeling embarrassed as she squinted, sucking her teeth. He figured it was a good time to apologize, since she'd finally caught him face to face.

"What's up?" she spat back, as he smiled, slowly dragging his hand down his mouth. "Let's start with how and why you did me like that, Denver? It was that bad?" she fussed, coming outside like she was ready to fight with no shoes on.

"Aye, shorty, chill," he said, laughing as he shook his head. "A nigga was messed up back then, and before anyone caught feelings, I had to beat it, baby girl," he told her, watching her perky breasts bounce up and down as her chest heaved up and down.

"Caught feelings? Feelings were already caught—mine. You think I fuck inmates for fun?" she challenged him, staring him up and down.

"Shit, to be honest, I figured you did. I barely even spoke to you," he told her, catching an attitude himself when she started to cry. He wasn't expecting that at all. Not when he figured she'd moved on to the next man or inmate—whichever one it was. "Fuck," he groaned, sighing. "Come here," he told her, opening up his arms as she pouted and sniffled. "Shit, alright then," he said, waving her off when she crashed against his chest, almost knocking him down.

"I-I'm sorry," she whimpered. He wasn't sure what she was apologizing about but instead of drudging up the past, he decided to do something different. That was be quiet. Women were emotional beings and even though he never really cared how she felt back then, for some reason, he cared now. Being free did something to him. That and seeing her in distress. "I came at you all wrong. I-I was just hurt. I thought we were cool, though," she released, swiping at her tear-filled rimmed eyes.

"Damn right we was. Good pussy having self," he teased, causing her to suck her teeth and laugh. "I mean, it was straight, but on the real. Level up, baby girl. Don't let a man fuck on you like that, that can't do nothing for you. I was on my ass. You're smart, funny, and you have heart. I see you," he said, looking at her house. It wasn't extravagant or anything but it was hers. "Stepping out and finally doing your own thing despite your daddy means you believe in yourself. Now execute that shit at all times," he told her, lifting her chin as he looked at her with authority. "Alright?"

"Alright," she told him, taking a deep breath as a faint smile appeared. "Does that mean we can't at least be friends?" she couldn't help but ask when he chuckled, releasing her. "Just friends, I promise," she said, holding up both hands. "Trust me, I'm not even tripping off the past."

"Good, because I had no business fucking you then anyway."

"And now?" she asked, quickly double talking as she took in his bowed legs and third muscle that rested with ease against his leg. She saw he was buffer than he was a few years before, a tad bit darker too, but she wasn't hating at all. If he could lift her then, certainly he could lift her now and onto his face if she were asked where she wanted to sit in that moment. "I'm sorry." She laughed. "That was so thirsty, but at one time, I did drink from the cup of Denver before… right?"

"Dashon, girl, you're a trip," was all he said. Then his dick jumped, making him rethink her "friends only" offer.

"I did, but now, I'm just trying to do me. No relationships, just new beginnings. Thus, the starter home I paid for with *my* money and this jacked up yard. A young juvenile corrections officer's pay ain't much, but it's mine."

"Following in your father's footsteps?"

"No, but it's a start, and I like working with the youth. So let's start over. I'm Dashon Ivory, and I have no clue what happened with this yard before I moved here. Give me a new estimate," she said, shocking him.

"We can," he said, admiring how quickly she rebounded. It was clear she had a lot going on, and while with no ill intent on his part, he'd made it worse. "Matter a fact"—he said, fishing out his cell—"I want us to do that over lunch. Go shower and put on something. Let's grab something to eat so we can catch up. Besides, I can see you're grumpy when food deprived," he slid in, teasing her. When he did, a light snicker escaped her lips as she rolled her eyes.

"So you're being nice after I was being an asshole?"

"Hey, I'm a nice guy, and I was being one first sort of when I cut you off a few years ago. But on the real, this job right here is going to cost you more. And without checking, the sprinklers probably don't work, but later for that, Ms. Ivory."

"Twenty minutes?" she said, hoping that wasn't too long to wait. "You can even come in. I have water, tea, and lemonade." When she said lemonade, Denver laughed. "What?"

"Nothing. Water's just fine," he said, stepping inside before she closed the door. "Fine ass," he said to himself, reminiscing about her thick now toned thighs but more importantly, her smile. It was huge and contagious, one that had him smiling even after she'd walked away.

"Let me chill," he told himself. He made it a habit never to play where he made money or where it could affect his money. If anything, he'd learned that from working for the Valentines, something he'd never do again since he planned to stay the fuck out of their way.

Chapter Seven

"Breaking news, Grammy Award winning gospel and R&B singer, Razz Streeter, was located on the island of Punta Cana, and he wasn't with his wife. Oh no. Check out those photos. That's the Streeters' makeup and hair stylist, Amber Rhinestone. While we haven't received a comment from the Streeter camp, we have been told that his wife, singer, songwriter and musician, Faith Streeter, was seen leaving Paris late last week. I don't know about you, but I'd pick being on a beach in sunny Punta Cana than Paris where it's wet and cool," radio host Seagal Simon said as he laughed.

"Please, just like a man to choose the woman that's the twenty while the woman that gave him one hundred is out being about her business. Trust, Faith wasn't lollygagging around in Paris shopping for bags. She is the bag," his co-host, Ryda Rose chimed in, sucking her teeth. "Everyone knows that Faith is the muscle and brain in that marriage and behind their success. She's sitting in boardrooms making deals while he's sipping from the likes of their assistant."

"Makeup and hairstylist, ma'am. She was making up the hair he'd

just messed up," Seagal countered as the room filled with a chorus of laughs from producers.

"Well, she's going to need more than that because I'm sure that ride she had with the Streeters is over."

"Oh, are you sure?" Seagal posed, pursing his lips like the diva he was. "I think she's riding Razz just fine. Maybe it's the wife that needs to sit on something besides a board," he added, clapping his hands.

"Hmph, maybe she has. I'm just saying," Ryda implied. "Razz may have stepped down while the Faith Streeter I know, with her bad self, outgrew him. Trust, I'm sure she's somewhere like me, unbothered."

"Tell 'em, girl," Faith spat at the radio, shaking her head. "I need to send Ryda something for being a sweetie. As for that Seagal, fu—" she said then caught herself, staring at the church in front of her. "Well, you know what I mean," she whispered in frustration, looking up at the sky.

She'd been driving for hours, and the sky looked how she felt—dark and dreary. At least on the inside because if nothing else, Faith Streeter stayed dressed to the nines as if cameras were snapping like fireworks somewhere far off, even in the small town of Mason.

"You seem bothered to me, girlfriend," Seagal fired back, snapping his fingers.

He just wouldn't let up, and then she remembered why. She'd curved him a few years back before he revealed his sexuality. He was only trying to come up when she was rising to the top. Now they were all gay or bisexual, albeit it was better than being on the downlow in the industry. She wasn't homophobic by any stretch of the imagination. Neither was Razz, but she smelled snake all over Seagal from the moment he said hello and now his bitchness bellowed loudly behind a mic.

"Faith, if you're listening, Razz needs to go and play somewhere safe like behind the scenes. Make a statement, and shut the buzz down, baby

girl. In the meantime, I got you," *Ryda sang in the mic, sticking her tongue out.*

"Pfft," was all Seagal said, yet looking to see the lines light up. He was silently praying Razz did mess up. Then maybe he could see if Razz were in the downlow club.

"Yup, keep that same silent energy while I do this," Ryda said as Ciara's "Level Up" came booming through the air.

Once Faith turned the radio off, she went to her cell, quickly shooting Joy a text message to have something sent to the station for Ryda. Since she'd cut off her publicist and entire industry family, Joy had become her unofficial assistant. After she caught her masturbating in a deep, sensually and sexually charged sexscapade with Denver in her sleep, Joy demanded that she leave in search of healing and recovering what life seemed to have stolen from her. For the first time in her life she did something selfish, something just for her.

"God." She sighed, feeling overwhelmed. For the first time in years, she was alone. Alone, alone. So alone, she didn't even feel God. She took a few deep breaths, praying that the Almighty didn't strike her down, especially since she hadn't stepped a foot in church in more than three years unless it was to perform. While they started out singing gospel, in no time, Razz had pulled her into his life. Soon, they sold their soul to the devil, releasing a few R&B albums where Razz showcased his rapping skills. While Faith still gave God praise, her heart wasn't in it. Just like she'd somehow left God, it seemed like he'd left her too.

From time to time, she still wrote music for gospel artists and even for herself, but she hated to admit that R and B music paid more. And sadly, it also paid for the lifestyle that made her net worth thirty million, which more than its fair share went back home early on in her career to help out with the expenses at Piney Grove Ministries. Seems like her father's problems had been fixed as their new worship center was the size of an arena and her parents lived in a thirty thousand square foot home one could get lost in.

Once she heard the rumble of thunder in the background after a streak of lighting, she snapped out of her thoughts and unlocked the door. Several parishioners, like her, were seen quickly exiting their vehicles. Unlike them, though, who smiled and waved at others as they passed them by, Faith felt dead inside and full of gloom.

"God, what are you trying to tell me?" she whispered, looking up at the dark gray sky. She still asked, even though she wasn't expecting an answer. Still, asking him was better than trusting her own poor judgement, which got her to where she was in the first place. There was plenty of money, but love felt foreign, even absent. It had been like that since Denver and the only people that were happy was her father and Razz.

"I guess only time will tell, huh?" she answered herself, slipping her shades on as she stepped out of her Tesla. Gone were her thick long tresses of wavy hair, as she rocked a short cut with golden highlights and Gucci shades. She was taking a bit of a risk moving around without security, but at this point, she just didn't care.

She needed to hear a word from God and fast.

Chapter Eight

"That's why I wanted her earlier this week, Day," Denver said to his daughter's mother, trying to wrap the conversation up. "Well, I didn't know I had to ask for permission to travel with my kid."

Dumb ass girl, he thought as his grandmother looked him in the face, daring him to curse.

"And besides, you know how I move. The last thing on my mind is a woman. If I'm out of pocket, trust and believe, ma, it's always about business," he explained, shaking his head.

As his grandmother listened on, she prayed he'd find a way to make peace before Dashon would threaten him again about not seeing his daughter. That was the only time and way she could get him to acquiesce when it came to her demands, but as of late, especially after he'd reconnected with God, even that wasn't working like it used to.

His grandmother begged him to focus on himself as soon as he brought Dashon home weeks after they'd reconnected, especially when she learned of their history and things Dashon had done to get attention. She wasn't judging, but any woman that had no regard for her own father's career was damaged goods. She needed the Lord, not a man, and certainly not a child from one who lacked the capacity to love her back. She was falling nowhere fast while their daughter was stuck in the middle.

"Then next week I'm getting her. Shit, it's simple then," he said when his grandmother slapped his arm. "Grams, chill." He laughed. "I keep telling you I'm a grown man," he said, grinning when she slapped him again.

"I don't care how grown you think you are. You won't talk like you're in the streets in front of me. And don't you have somewhere to be?" she asked him loudly, hoping Dashon overhead their conversation.

"Yeah, alright, Grams," he said, nodding his head, while Dashon rambled on about his grandmother disliking her.

He was fuming, praying she didn't say one disrespectful thing about his grandmother. If she did, damn church. He was gunning for her head straight on I-99, headed to Jonestown. He never once felt he'd bargained for a life sentence *after prison*, but that's exactly what he received when he ended up getting her pregnant. That ultimatum she historically liked issuing to men didn't work either. The only difference between him and Roger was he'd put a baby up in her right around the time she did.

"Alright, Day. Check your account. I gotta slide to church."

"Money isn't the answer to everything, Denver," his grandmother warned him, rolling into the kitchen behind him once he got off the phone. She usually attended church with him, but the rain made her joints ache. Denver couldn't get into live streaming, his attention shorter than a gnat on crack. So he pressed on, even getting up early to work out before church.

Gone was the lanky, six-foot-tall boy who'd left his family behind before prison, as he easily stood almost six three weighing two hundred pounds. With tatted, toned arms and thick, bowed legs, he easily drew the attention of women, especially church women, prepared to slip in as soon as service started dressed in a burgundy Italian three-piece suit he had custom made.

He wasn't selling dope anymore and, thankfully, he didn't have to. His love for gardening and cutting lawns birthed out of his desire just to be around Faith years ago had paid off nicely since his own landscaping company had grown to include residential and commercial contracts in and outside of Jonestown. He was easily grossing seventy five grand a more a month and it wasn't slowing down anytime soon it seemed with a team of thirty employees.

"Grams, please," he said, waving her off. "Money answers all things, right?" he teased, using her biblical references she'd spat in a heartbeat against her. "Ecclesiastes ten and nineteen."

"Hmph. Move on over to first Timothy six and ten. The *love* of it can be deadly and destructive," she quipped, swatting at him. "Now go on, and don't let me tell you again. You know I don't play about being late to the Lord's house when he's always right on time for us. And Ida is picking me up after my service goes off," she reminded him, speaking of one of her friends back in Jonestown.

"Why even come here if you're leaving so soon, Grams?"

"Boy, don't you question me, but to answer your question, they're having their annual summer explosion at Piney Grove," she said, referring to one of the still most talked about church events in all of Jonestown.

"Yeah, that," he mumbled, shaking his head as a gang of

text messages came in from Dashon. She was miserable… miserable and scorned. No way was he marrying her or stepping foot in her parents' home. They'd fucked their daughter's head up, so the way he saw it, they should pay for her clinical care. *Broad's a straight whack job*, he thought to himself.

Once the warden discovered they were together, he never made it easy for Denver anyhow. He treated him like he was still locked down too, demanding information he felt only his daughter should share. Over time, Denver had told him to fuck off and suck a dick like it was rumored on the prison yard. He stayed watching him like a hawk, making Denver feel like he'd have to resort to his old ways by sending his daughter's grandfather on to glory.

"Don't start. Since Faith and that husband of hers have made it big, they don't even perform anymore."

"Why you telling me that?" he shot back, grabbing his keys after finishing off a muffin. He never ate too much before church out of fear of going to sleep, but he planned to eat as soon as church was out. Since his grandmother was leaving, he figured he slide by Nana's, a local southern joint, that served all the southern fixings for a single man like himself. "And here," he said, pressing money in her hand. "I don't need Ida trying to steal my grams by buying her shit she thinks I won't. I heard you talking about how cheap I am." He laughed.

"Curse again, boy. I'll whoop your juvenile delinquent ass," she fussed as he kissed her once more on the cheek, laughing as he headed out the door.

Chapter Nine

Looking in the mirror, Faith blinked her bloodshot eyes in the church's bathroom. She'd just made it in before the rain came rushing down. Bloodshot from crying and definitely from the lack of sleep as she gently touched her slick edges. She'd gone for the wet and wild look that accentuated her cheekbones and chinky eyes. She had to admit the highlights set it off, but she was unsure how long she'd keep the look. For now, going unnoticed, proved that it worked.

She wasn't sure what truly led her to Mason, but once Joy smoked her out of her condo, she saw that as a sign she needed to leave and make amends with God. This time, however, she wasn't going to her mother or father, the ones who groomed her to love and serve the Lord. She had plans to seek forgiveness for many things, but one was not living in her truth.

"On the road? When? And what happened with going off to school? You already put off one semester," Faith's mother asked her, totally confused.

"Mama... Razz needs me," she whispered. He made her turn her back not only on her dreams, but her family too. Well, her mother and sisters, it seemed. Said it was good for the both of them and she believed him. He'd done a complete one eighty and somehow, slipped into her heart. "And God has shown him favor. Look at what he's done for us and Piney Grove Ministries. Heck, even Jonestown. He trusts no one but me when it comes to music. I want to help keep him focused, Mama. This is huge for all of us."

"Keep him focused, Faith? By being what? His chaperone? Baby—" her mother said, feeling anxious inside. "He's a grown man. Now, don't get me wrong. I love Razz, and he's definitely a gift to the body of Christ, but putting your dreams on hold... I don't know," she told her, as history seemed to be repeating itself. A sacrifice was being made yet again and in the name of what she was sure was a blind love. A love she'd spent years trying to recover from in her own loveless marriage.

After following her husband, the great Pastor Theodore Valentine, she too gave up her dream of playing classical music all over the world. After he wore her down and suckered her out of a date, within a year after graduating from college they were married, and within two years, they had their first child.

"I love music, Mama. Always have, you know that. It's in me, and because it is, it will never go away. Besides, who needs me there when Brother Taron has been doing an amazing job. Heck, even Sister Mary catches the holy ghost before the bridge," she teased, hoping it helped, although it didn't.

"Mama? Mama, you still there?" she asked, the same defeat and gloom her mother felt now running through her veins.

"Yes, child. I'm here," she whispered with tightly shut eyes, silently praying. Her husband had been out of town for days, and her girls were still asleep. She always slept lightly whenever he wasn't home, so the call from Faith scared her, praying no one was in trouble or hurt.

"I'm right on this one, Mama, and ministering to the Lord comes in different ways. I'm still doing that helping Razz with this new album. The record company has already heard a few of the songs I've written and composed. I'm telling you, God is moving mightily," she said excitedly as her mother shook her head no, silently disagreeing.

"Yes he is, Faith, but remember this, my child. God is not the author of confusion. When he shows up, things must be done in decency and in order. I just pray this is the hand of God and not that of the enemy," she told her, wondering just how long this plan had been in motion. "Next thing you're going to tell me is that you're married."

"Well..." she said and paused, looking over at Razz. His jaw twitched as he tightly gripped the steering wheel. He didn't have to hear her mother's side of the conversation to know that congratulations weren't in order about her abandoning her own path. That and the fact that her mother always seemed to go hard for Denver, even after he was long gone.

"God, no," she gasped. "Faith Valentine, your father is going to be very upset," she spat in a panic. She had to call him and fast so he could remind their child that she still lived under their roof and had to live by their rules.

"Mama, it was him that married us," was all she said before her mother passed out and woke up hours later in her own urine.

By the time the pastor started whooping and hollering and the air filled with a chorus of amens, Faith was sprawled out on the floor in tears. One second, she was angry with God and her father, the next at herself and her mother, a mother who never seemed to hold her father accountable. She needed protection; she deserved it, and all she felt now was abandoned, taken advantage of, and alone.

Thankfully, she wore a long pencil skirt and a satin, choker collared top where a bow rested in front of her chest. It was blue, a powder blue that complemented a bone-colored wrap that was the same color as her skirt. Once the spirit consumed her and her legs gave way, that wrap quickly covered her legs. She was sure it was one of the ushers who'd placed it there, knowing legs on a church floor was almost seen as a sin.

She cried out to God with her eyes closed until she heard a whisper of a voice that shook the core of her soul. And not just any voice. It was one she hadn't heard in more than seven years. It was husky, yet soft as it echoed and spoke to the ache in her heart. Her body stiffened when he said, "I got her. She's always good with me."

God, is that you? Do-do you sound like him? Am I dead? Is he dead? she asked herself, afraid to move with tightly pinched eyes. Unlike the night at Joy's, she was sure this wasn't a dream. Mostly because they were inside of a church, and she smelled that smell. That wood-scented fragrance that swooped in and woke up all of her nerve endings.

Oh, God. It's really him.

His hands then arms slid underneath her body and lifted her up, causing her to remember the first day he'd ever touched her body and then her soul. It was the day where the wasp had stung her, and the day he'd captured her heart. As he began to walk, it seemed as if his feet were pushing on top of clouds as he carried her with ease. He treated her as if she were fragile, just like a delicate flower that needed attending to.

When she couldn't hold it in anymore, tears rained down her face as she released a wail that pierced his heart. Her arms slipped around his neck as she cried out to God. She cried out to Denver too, asking him and God to forgive her as he shushed her while gently rubbing her back.

She didn't realize how much she missed him, craved him until that moment as she begged him to never let her go. His touch, his feel, his smell. Hell, him period. The feel of his stubble from his lightly shaven face against hers made her hold onto him even tighter as tears saturated his neck, shirt, and chest.

She whimpered, overjoyed from the feel of the pad of his thumb against her cheek as he found a seat next to him and lowered her body down. When he did, she felt the texture of his calloused hands. Calloused from hard years of labor, that soon swiped and smoothed the hair out of her face.

After he did, she felt his body shake from digging in his pocket where he produced a handkerchief. One that smelled like him as he dabbed her eyes, then whispered, "Blow."

And she did just that.

"It's really you?" she whispered, her eyes searching his face etched with pain. No matter how hard he masked his emotions, when it came to Faith, that's all he was—a walking mass of emotions.

"Denver. I, I—"

"Shhhh," he replied, interrupting her. "Not now, Mouse," he cautioned her, easily slipping into hold habits as he called her by the nickname he'd given her years earlier. A name her husband despised. "Not now," he said, unsure if he could maintain his composure if she dared to utter another word. Her presence alone was overwhelming, consuming so much so, he hated she still had that effect on him.

As the service continued, Denver relaxed just a little as his hold around her body remained intact, basking in the feel of her skin and smell. Even in her hair. Each time she fidgeted or moved, he prayed she'd stop out of fear of lifting her up and taking her with him where he'd punish her mercilessly with his dick. She still smelled the same, a scent of lemon and honey dancing and seeping into his nose. All he could do was think of her and their past, some good times, some bad.

The good begging him to hold onto her and never let her go while the bad telling him to run and cast any thought of her into a sea of forgetfulness. Still, this was Faith, his Mouse, and maybe it was God's way of telling them both it was time they dealt with their past.

Chapter Ten

"Why did you give up on us so easily back then?" she blurted out.

"You know… before all that other stuff."

After church, they took a silent stroll to her car when he asked her if she was hungry. He wasn't prepared to let her go just yet, and he could tell she had no real place to go. A first in years as she looked around seemingly unsure of what to do next. Once her stomach growled lightly answering for her, off to midday brunch they went.

Minutes later, they pulled in front of the southern cuisine café, Nana's, the place where he'd planned to go before their paths crossed. It was known for serving up Mason's infamous salmon croquette, shrimp, and cheese grits dish with a side of blueberry waffles. The smell alone had Faith's mouth salivating. She couldn't wait to get inside and now they'd been served, it seemed her appetite had somehow dissipated.

"Honestly?" he replied and shook his head, stirring his grits. The other stuff, he assumed, was his prison stint. It was something he still wasn't comfortable discussing. Not with her or anyone. He'd done his time like a man and never snitched on a soul about anything. Still, it didn't mean that he didn't feel slighted about how things had turned out.

"I remember the first time I saw you, I mean *really* saw you," he said instead, choosing to start off with something that made him smile. He leaned back and grinned, remembering how smitten he was the first time he saw her. Her mocha-colored skin with slanted, chink like eyes that almost disappeared when she smiled.

"Really, Denver?" she asked with a lift of her brows, before sitting back and releasing air from her mouth. He was deflecting, tossing her inquiry to the side which was the only thing that mattered to her. Instead of calling him on it, Faith found herself rolling with it like she'd done with many other things in her life as he decided to walk down a lighter memory lane of theirs.

"Yeah," he said as he chin checked her, daring her to stop him. She'd heard this story before, too many times from her sisters over the years. Yet, even now, hearing it again never seemed to grow old.

"Like I was saying, here comes little teeny tiny Faith Valentine, walking inside the church. Happy, too." He laughed, rubbing the back of her hand, the coarseness creating goosebumps that were hard for either of them to ignore. "Hell, I'm still wondering how your head held up those two big ponytails that flopped up and down as the music played," he continued, chuckling lowly.

"Oh, hush it," she interjected, tucking her lips in as she fought hard not to smile.

"I'm saying though," he told her, looking at her as he tilted his head. "Your head is kind of big," he teased yet noticed the golden highlights she was rocking. It was different for her. Different but good, and she was just as beautiful as always. Yet he wasn't sure if she even recognized her own beauty or how it was viewed from his eyes as he saw the beauty on the inside screamed even louder. Always did if he were being honest. Sure, he'd fallen for her looks, but he'd sunk like a ship when it came to her heart. Faith was everything in the world to him back then and it seemed even now.

"No bigger than yours," she shot back with a snort, blushing. He'd noticed that too. That's what she did whenever she was in his presence—blushed. "The infamous Denver Daniels. All the girls loved you, wanted you—"

"Yet only one had me," he spoke, cutting her off. "Got my ass whooped too behind you. I couldn't help it though. Shorty bust up in church with this cool ass sunflower dress. I had to get at them flowers," he said, looking intently in her eyes. No one had ever acted so boldly, so recklessly about her or for her, stealing flowers from the church's ground, then giving them to her. He was thirteen, and one who had fucked plenty of girls yet only wanted one—Faith Valentine.

He wanted to say more, but he didn't, watching her as she slid down in the chair. His eyes boring deeply into hers caused her to fidget before she steered her eyes away, clearing her throat.

She's nervous, he thought, smiling. Admittedly, he was too, but unlike her, he'd learned to mask his feelings over the years. Well, almost.

"Yeah, un huh." He nodded. "It was always like that when it came to you. Stop pretending I didn't mess hard with you, Mouse," he said as she cracked a smile. "Then there was mean ass Mercy who'd come in right bchind you with Joy's feisty behind. They'd be cutting up, pushing all on each other. Yet you were cool as a fan, proudly leading the Valentine preacher kids' pack," he said, noticing her misty eyes when her eyes danced up his face and back into his eyes.

"That's how you saw me? Cool as a fan?" she whispered nervously, rolling and fidgeting the napkin in her hands. Her hands were clammy, feeling that heat, that same passion she'd always felt whenever he was around.

"I mean, yeah," he responded with a slight shrug, fighting hard not to shift to a dark place. He missed that reaction, needed it as she dangled love in his face. He didn't need her love. Her love crippled him, yet he couldn't help it when he gave in. "Still are."

"That was sweet of you," she released softly.

"Me, sweet?" He laughed, his jaw twitching as it was him this time that had looked away. She heard him grunt, a sign of frustration before he sat back and glared at her, his eyes steely and dark. She knew then he was angry yet confused as to why when it was clear that it was him that had broken things off with her.

"You know what, never mind," she said, sitting up and sighing. "You don't have to *explain* anything to me," she said, with a sarcastic smile. "I have no right asking. Heck, look at my life. I'm rich, right? What problems do I have?" She laughed, tearing up as he fought hard not to agree with her.

Sadly, there were parts of him that felt he didn't owe her shit, then other parts that wanted to tell her how devastated he was living a life where she didn't exist. Still, life was different now. They were two different people, living two different lives. Her with a husband and him with a daughter.

Yet and still, when it came to Faith, his Mouse, Denver's usual hard demeanor began to wane. Even all these years later, her presence tugged on his mental and definitely his heart.

"It's cool," he pushed out, deciding to let it go before they went down memory lane any further.

"Yeah," she quickly agreed. "It's cool. We can enjoy breakfast, then I go my way and you go yours. No harm, no foul. No need in trying to figure out the what, when, or why about who didn't get what they wanted or deserved. Just leave after our little kumbaya and never look back," she replied, infuriated at how dismissive he was being, which didn't go unnoticed.

Her spoiled fucking ass. Always has to get what she wants, he thought to himself, laughing as he took in the scowl on her face. He was sick of her shit, her family's shit, and anyone else who felt he had to bow down to their demands. Not when he'd done nothing but come home and moved on with his life. *Fucking nerve of her.*

"What?" she said, fuming as she pushed out a light chuckle. That laugh finally pushed him over the edge, as he leaned forward and smiled, resting his elbows on the table. The space between them lessened when he did.

"You sure you want an 'honest for your ass' answer?" he asked her, deciding to go for it, unleashing the beast inside of him. The beast that needed to hurt her like she'd hurt him.

"Sure, why not?" she replied with that same laugh, picking up her glass of orange juice as she took a cutesy sip. The kind that came with a soft slurp as she batted her eyes that he'd fought hard to ignore.

"Cool, Mouse. Let me enlighten you then," he said, issuing a wicked smile that made her skin crawl but surprisingly made her pussy jump at the same time. It was insane, fucking insane as she gushed at his perfectly white teeth. White teeth that he slid his tongue across which caused her to squirm. "You good?" he whispered, sliding his tonguc across his tceth once more.

"Who, me?" she asked, feigning a look of confusion. "Pfft. I'm very good. I'm waiting on you," she told him, scooping up a spoon full of eggs and bouncing her leg as if she had no care in the world.

"Yeah, okay," he replied, smiling as he nodded his head. If she wanted to play, he came to play. That included not sparing her feelings at all, especially since she hadn't spared his feelings the day it was her, from his recollection, that decided to end things.

"Look, I know shit got too hot for you, and since we're keeping it real *today*, I'll be honest," he said with a shrug. "I didn't expect you to stick around," he confessed, matter of factly. "Why would you? The pastor's daughter, a Valentine at that, with talent and big dreams, coming to see a convict? You had a whole fucking career ahead of you, and what did I have? Seven years. Seven fucking years where you would sit across the table eating bullshit ass food from the vending machine. Oh, and let's not forget hours of riding to and from, tolls included, only to be eye fucked in a room full of niggas that didn't give a fuck about you being mine," he seethed, with clenched fists, as her eyes bucked wide.

"Naw, why stick around when you got yourself a fucking boy toy? One that would shuck and dance for you and your father and on stage," he added. "I can't lie." He laughed. "Once he was all cleaned up, he did fit the image. Good ole Pastor Valentine wasted no time doing that. Cleaned him up, begged Jesus to help get him into heaven, then turned around and gave my fucking woman to him… and you *let* him," he released, his voice heavily laced with venom that made her eyes blink in disbelief. "Yeah, you let him, Mouse."

"Denver," she replied in forced whisper, looking around. "This is crazy. I'm telling you I—"

"Naw, Mouse. Let a nigga finish," he said, smiling that same smile as she fought back tears. "I told you, I get it. Besides, what did I expect? For them to escort me in shackles down to one of your shows or on the red carpet?" He laughed. "Naw, fuck that. So, instead of asking me why I walked, ask your fucking self who really did the walking because what I just described I never got a chance to experience locked up or not, *Faith Streeter.* Oh, did I mention you gave up college and my pussy too?" he told her, daring her to cry her way out of that.

If she wanted this side, this heat, then he was committed to giving it to her as her mouth fell wide open, tears slowly trickling down her face as whispers were heard from the patrons nearby.

"What?" He smiled, looking around at others who were looking at them. "Mind your fucking business," he snarled.

"Wow," she whispered, sniffling as he waved her off.

"Girl, fuck these people," he told her. "And what? That is your last name. The fuck I look like explaining to you why I didn't chase a motherfucker that basically left me for dead. Wrote me one fucking letter, telling me it's over and then removing yourself from the visitation list."

"Are you fucking serious? That's your 'honest for your ass' answer?" she spat, slamming her hands on the table. "Before I even address the letter and visitation part, let me respond to set the record straight, and don't you say one fucking word," she seethed.

"Look at Mouse bossing up." He laughed.

"Shut up. Just shut up!" she warned him, her voice trembling when she looked around. "And that means you all too," she told the couple next to them, sucking her teeth. When she did, Denver's heart dropped as he swallowed slow and hard.

He'd never seen Faith like this, this enraged, this angry. He was speechless.

"Me going to college or anywhere without you was *never* an option. Mmkay?" she replied, sassily swiping the tears away with one hand. "As for me even eating bullshit ass food, I'd do it standing on my head if I could eat bullshit ass food *with you*," she fussed, spittle flying in the air. "And I wouldn't care about sitting in a room full of inmates, because all I would see is you. Even when I didn't see you, smell you, feel you, or heard your voice, I still wanted you. And the sad thing is I still do now. So don't you dare pretend that I cut you off… *Rock*," she hissed, using his street name as she hit him below the belt. "As for the letter, I never fucking wrote it, and it was *you* that took *me* off that list. Yeah, now take my 'honest for your ass' response."

"Bullshit," he fumed, snatching up a napkin and wiping his mouth. "Don't fucking play with me, Mouse. A nigga was stuck, and you moved around like I didn't even exist. Like I said"—he smiled—"cool as a fan."

"You know what?" she said, pushing her chair back and standing up. "Fuck you. Ma'am, the bill, please?" she called out to their waitress who stood nearby in shock. "Oh, and I'm paying for both," she told her before she looked his way. "I want to make sure history says that this time I for damn sure didn't run out on you without paying for my share and yours."

"The fuck you are," he spat, fishing his wallet out and slapping his credit card on the table. "I'm good on taking anything else from a Valentine."

"Oh, I thought I was a Streeter," she replied, tilting her head and batting her eyes. "Funny thing is that I was told it was *you* that took me off that visitation list and got me banned from the prison. So fuck you, Denver. At least be a man about it."

"I did what?" he replied, rage coursing throughout his body. "Yo, that's funny, Mouse. Imagine me doing that, having the gorilla balls to even do some foul ass shit like that. That's crazy." He laughed until he realized she wasn't laughing at all. She was crying, her body trembling as she took deep and long breaths, fanning her face. The longer he stood there watching her fall apart, the more he began to realize someone else had their hand in this as she turned around to leave.

"The fuck you going, Mouse?' he growled, grabbing her by her hand and stopping her. No way was she dropping that kind of information on him and leaving. Not when there wasn't an ounce of truth to it.

"Where you want me to go. Away, Denver. I'm finally giving you what you wanted, but at least we get to say it to each other face to face," she released through gritted teeth as his hold on her wrist tightened.

"Mouse, ma," he whispered, emotions at an all-time high as he pulled her toward him. When her body crashed into his, she felt the walls of pent-up frustration tumbling down the more determined he became to not let her go. "This time, *no one* is going any got damn where. Sit the fuck down and talk, or I'll make you," he warned her, his mouth against her ear as the waitress returned.

"Can I get you two uh, anything else?" she asked, watching him pull back before he rested his forehead against Faith's. She wasn't sure if they were still fighting or about to have a full-fledged make out session. It was so intense, so passionate, she began to wonder if she should just leave.

"Ask the lady," he whispered, his nose then lips grazing hers. Her eyes fluttered when they did, before he surprisingly pecked her mouth. "Because anything she wants from me from here on out, she can have it," he said, smiling which was short-lived. "I mean that shit, Mouse. Ask for anything, and it's yours."

He had no clue what he was doing. He just knew he didn't want to do it without her, no matter who her husband was.

"Including getting rid of that bullshit ass husband so you can fuck with a bullshit ass convict," he added, releasing a bit of tension they managed to build up so quickly as she grinned. "Yeah, that's what I like to see. I want to see my Mouse smile, ole crybaby ass. I knew that fucking crying was that kryptonite that soon would break a nigga down," he told her.

"Hush," was her weak comeback as he pecked her mouth once more.

"Any questions?" he asked her, inhaling her scent. He was prepared to push all their food off that table and feast on her pussy and would have if he felt that wouldn't have gotten them arrested.

"N-no. No questions," she replied, blushing and sniffling. He gently tilted her head up by the chin with his index finger. A grin appeared as he took all of her beauty in, even with red, puffy eyes and a swollen nose. She was still his Mouse and always would be.

"Good, now that we got these 'honest for your ass' answers out the way, let me show you something."

"Wait, about the letter and list. Who would have done that?" she asked, hurt and confused.

"Mouse, I don't know, but we'll figure that shit out together," he told her. "Just don't leave. Stay and kick it with me for another day."

"I think I have a few days, if you'll have me," she added, her voice filled with hope. Truth was she had as many days as he wanted or needed to keep feeling what she felt.

"A few, huh?" he asked, feeling the same. It was like old times, times where they connected as if no one else mattered.

He was so caught up in the moment, he'd forgotten to share one small detail. That was him being a father, because this time, he was playing for keeps and Razz would feel his wrath.

Chapter Eleven

"How do you plan to fix this, Raziel?" his father-in-law asked him as they sat in his private jet. Raziel was going nuts behind Faith's hiatus.

Calls for shows, interviews, and endorsements were coming in, to which she not only offered guidance on but would reject if it didn't match their brand. She might have not been the wife he ran home to fuck, but she was definitely more than a performer and song writer. Faith was a musical genius and a beast of a businesswoman.

"She won't talk," he said, speaking of Amber. They'd met on a video shoot Faith missed out on, handling other business, two years ago. While just friends for some time, they'd ran into each other at an industry afterparty. He'd just won two Dove awards, one being song of the year which Faith had written and then album of the year which bore her name on most of the songs. Before the night was over, she and his wife were huddled up laughing and talking. By the time they'd left to head to their hotel rooms, she and Faith exchanged numbers, and a friendship was born. Soon, that morphed into a job or two before she brought her on fulltime and, unknowingly, into her bedroom with her husband.

"And you would know this because?" he asked him, shaking his head. "Have you not learned anything over the years, Raziel?"

"She has too much to lose," he assured him as he nodded his head in deep thought, especially after he made her cut off anyone in the entertainment industry when it came to makeup and hair styling. At first it was to keep their dealings private, limit any opportunity for their affair to be detected. But now, he knew it was more. Razz had somehow fallen in love with another woman.

"Besides, it was nothing," he lied with ease, his shades hiding the deceit in his eyes. "One too many mimosas that morning. We were just kicking back and enjoying the scenery. Like I said, it was nothing."

"Hmph. These don't look like nothing, Raziel," he replied, tossing his cell that showed the photos of Amber on Razz's lap. "On the beach and only in her bikini bottoms while staring off into the sunset?"

"Aye, it was a nude beach," he spat, shrugging his shoulders. "Were we nude?"

"Do you have to be if the woman you're with is not your wife? Are you kidding me?"

"Faith was tired and didn't want to go. We'd just finished a ten-day shooting for the 'Behold Love' video in Paris. Everyone was just chilling, having a good time and… the top slipped off," he said, a light chuckle following.

"Oh, it slipped off and then your hands and lips somehow found their way on her shoulders, then down her breasts and stomach?" his father-in-law added facetiously as he leaned over in Raziel's face. "Oh, but wait," he said, swiping to the other photos. "You must have tried to help her put it back on except you used your mouth, you asshole," he spat, fuming. "Tugging on her hair and licking her neck. Is that the damn story you're sticking with? Jesus Christ, Raziel. All the while, Denver's sniffing up your wife's ass. Probably in your bed back home!" he barked when Razz's head snapped in his direction.

"The hell you say? Denver?" he repeated, snatching his shades off as he leaned forward. "What happened to seven years? If he caught that, he'd just be getting out. Either that, or you're sadly mistaken."

"You heard me. He's been out!" his father-in-law seethed, his chest heaving up and down.

He'd known for some time that Denver was out. It was all his grandmother talked about before she moved to Mason with him, but luckily for him and all of Piney Grove, Denver refused to step foot inside of their church. That didn't mean he hadn't made his presence known though.

He'd not only come home but had picked up right where he'd left off with his landscaping business that was now a reputable one all throughout Jonestown and surrounding areas. His company was the first name spoke of when it came to commercial contracts which were growing by the day. He was kicking his own ass pushing Faith to Razz when it seemed that overtime, Denver too, had found a way to provide for himself and rather well. Still, as long as their paths had never crossed and after he learned Denver had moved on with a woman and daughter, he felt no need to panic nor mention it to Razz or his daughter.

"Damn," he mumbled to himself, shaking his head. "What if… you know, someone starts talking? I was a kid."

"Trust me, money talks louder. You just worry about

Amber and getting your wife's ass back in your bed. I'll handle the rest," he assured him, standing up.

"Yeah, but are the streets talking?" he asked him, loosening his tie. Razz had long ago left a life of hustling behind him, but if he knew one thing that would always hold true was that if the streets were talking, he'd might have to watch his back. Even living the life of a celebrity.

"About you? Of course they are. Your dumb ass cheated on your wife, Raziel. The paparazzi is having a free for all while you or Faith refuse to make a statement."

"Tell me how I can when she won't even take my calls. Hell, she won't even take Rell's calls. Matter of fact, I think she changed her number," he said, chuckling as he angrily yanked off his tie.

Damn, Denver is out, he thought to himself as he fidgeted in his seat. He had security, plenty of it, but he also knew Denver. And because he did, he knew they too had unfinished business, business he was finishing up with his wife.

"And instead of trying to figure out why, you're on a jet headed to where?"

"To the meeting your daughter set up with Nigel Records. Just because she stopped working doesn't mean work stops," he replied, sliding his shades back on. He then noticed the look Rell gave him, one that said they'd be late if they didn't leave soon. He loved his wife, but he had other business to attend to. Business that would keep money coming in, and his father-in-law sitting there wasn't helping. He had not only his wife to provide for, but Amber too.

"Clearly, whatever she set up means she's working. She's *always* the one that showed up to work," he said, hinting at all the stunts Razz had pulled over the years. If he weren't talented, bringing in Piney Grove thousands of dollars over the years, he'd long ago would have had him blackballed. "So don't you dare make this about my child. In fact, I'm starting to think you screwing up isn't such a bad idea," he seethed, tugging on both sides of his jacket tightly. "Watch yourself, Raziel. Pride comes before destruction. Proverbs sixteen and eighteen," he quoted.

"Did that same scripture apply when you needed me… Dad?" he probed evilly as he smiled.

"Razz!" Rell called out. "Come on, bro. We're running late. Get your head in the game," he belted with authority. He'd done everything possible to keep things afloat in Faith's absence, but her father wasn't making it any easier. Like him, he too knew Denver was out long ago. He just knew telling Razz would only make things worse.

"Me too," his father-in-law spat irritated. "Unlike him, I have a church to run and a wife that's actually waiting for me. I'll be in touch, so keep your cell on and charged once you land. In the meantime, I have more cleaning up to do, *as usual.* And try screwing your wife for a change," he told him, bumping his leg as he exited the plane.

By the time the door closed, Razz exhaled. He not only had two women ignoring him, but he had an enemy doing God knows what with his wife. Rell sat next to him, quietly fuming as the pilot prepared them for takeoff. He'd made a choice himself a long time ago he felt was best for him. Years later, even he now wondered if choosing to work for Razz was the right choice.

"What?" Razz asked him with both hands lifted once Rell looked his way. "Look, if this is about Rock, fuck him. We're making a few million a show, and you're spooked about some washed up wannabe OG that's probably still out there trying to slang dope? Get the fuck out of here!" he released, still in shock about Denver breathing the same free air as him.

"I'm saying, Razz. Rock's name still has a lot of weight in streets and maybe with Faith. Washed up?" he said and paused, looking out the window. He didn't want to tell him how Denver's legal hustle was just as crazy if not crazier than how hard he pushed dope on the streets the last he'd heard.

"How the hell did those two link up?" Razz asked no one in particular before he answered himself. "Because Faith's ass is a hoe," he seethed angrily.

"Damn, man. That's your wife. That's cold," Rell told him, wondering when Razz would own the hand he played in Faith's disappearance then her reappearance with Denver.

He felt like he'd done everything he could over the years to be the man she needed him to be, became the gospel icon that sweated it out in the studio for hours on end right to the stage where they made some of the greatest hits and won numerous awards. He'd given her a better life than her father had given to her mother, causing him to kick the seat in front of him a few times before he barked, "That ungrateful ass bitch!"

"Razz, my man. Chill out with that hoe and bitch shit when it comes to Faith," Rell told him, sitting up as he looked his way.

"Why, you're fucking her too?"

"Aye, yo, Mr. Pilot. Let's get going before only one of us makes it..." he said and paused, looking at Razz ready to annihilate him. "And I guarantee you it will be me... nigga."

He loved Razz like a brother, but he loved Faith even more, especially when he learned about their union through the eyes of her sister, Joy. He'd never met the Razz Joy had described, but he was starting to wonder if maybe there were more sides to Razz that were now catching up with him.

He hoped not though, not when he chose following Razz on the road as head of security over starting a life with Joy. Even after she lashed out and professed she was dating a slew of men, he knew it was a lie and nothing but more lies she'd only told to hurt him.

She was and still would forever be his Joy Joy, his nickname for her.

"Whatever," Razz said, waving him off. "She has your ass fooled too. She definitely had my stupid ass. I should have let Rock keep her. I'm telling you she was probably putting money on that nigga's books, sucking dick too over the phone. How the fuck I know?" he roared.

"That's hella rude, yo. I'm serious. I'm warning you. Don't do sis like that," Rell seethed as the jet began to move. He was glad too or he was close to getting off.

"How? Is she here with me while we're trying to get this money? So what I fucked up and got caught? One time though, Rell?" he asked him, sounding illogical as Rell scrunched up his face. Especially since he'd gotten caught up quite a few times over the years. Just not publicly. "It's cool. Just find Amber because I'm real close to hiring a hitman for her ass. Faith can do whatever she wants, but Amber? Fuck no. Probably giving my pussy away," he spat stupidly while Rell sat back and shook his head.

"Matter of fact, I'm hiring one for both of my hoes," he added, kicking the seat in front of him once more. He was having a whole temper tantrum while both women seemed to have forgotten to kiss his ass.

Chapter Twelve

By the time they landed, Razz was sound asleep with no care in the world. As he slept, Rell pondered about the years he'd sat back and somehow had allowed money to become his God. He'd barely called home or even came home, and when he did, he was like Santa Claus, bearing gifts and tossing money at bitches in strip clubs or leaving it at their bedside. He did everything he could to not feel anything yet felt everything at the same time. He pushed the urge to quit more times than he'd care to admit, scrolling through social media while Joy lived her best life.

He even sat outside her parents' home many a nights drunk, calling her back to back, only for her to block him or wake up to find her gone with spray paint all over his truck. Joy was a motherfucker, one who didn't take shit from any of them— him, her parents, her sisters, or anyone.

He'd learned long ago that she'd rather suffer than dance to the beat of anyone's drum, including his, even if she danced all by herself with ten cents to her name. Joy Elaine Valentine could not and would not ever be bought. She lived on the street of "fuck you very much" which was right around the corner from "go to hell."

Rell laughed himself in stitches thinking about all the stunts she'd pulled over the years to get under his skin until he just stopped trying. She might have pretended it didn't matter, but he'd caught a few of her drunken rants on IG to know that it did. Still, until he knew he could give her what she wanted and deserved, he decided it was best to just leave her alone.

Seven years later, with Razz throwing his career and marriage away with no regard for anyone else, Rell decided it was time he dealt with his own unfinished business, and that was the youngest of the Valentine girls.

I need to see you, he texted Joy, praying she'd respond. Most times she didn't, but the last time he was sure he'd put a baby up in her, only to see her on Twitter rapping about another guy she was spending time with. He knew that was her lashing after he'd left her once again, so he blocked her and kept her on block… until now. *It's about sis*, he added, hoping that would help.

"Oh, shoot now," he whispered excitedly, as the three dots danced when she started responding. Razz had no clue about their dealings, despite a crush he confessed early on when they'd first met. He wasn't a broad, pillow talking his business and never would and he wanted to keep it that way too, standing up as he prepared to depart from the jet.

"Yo, get up," he told Razz, tapping him. "We're here. I need to hit the bathroom. The one in here is too tight for my big ass," he mumbled, walking off and leaving him on there.

Sis? Bitch, did my daddy have a son, she texted back, being sarcastic. He could even hear the sound of her voice, see her rolling her neck when she did as he read it.

"This fucking girl," he whispered to himself.

Joy Joy, it's all love over here. She's still my sis.

Funny, that love ain't felt this way. Faith gets a text though. Okay, Rellon, she texted back, using his real name.

Stop playing, Joy Joy. Never only about Faith. So what's up? Let me see you. It's important.

He was the only one that called her Joy Joy, causing her to smile. It didn't help she was high too, higher than two giraffes as she sat on her balcony, smoking and sipping on her margarita. She was horny too, close to telling him to come through and feed her some dick. But Rell was different, and not only because of his horse-sized package she called a trunk. It was heavy, thick and beautiful. Fucked her like she was a female elephant too, close to incapacitation with a smile on her face. No one ever made love to her body and her mind like Rell did, and she knew in her heart, no one ever would.

Still, she was aware that once she let him back into her life, she'd spend days, months, even years clawing him out of her heart. Their connection was just that intense, that toxic, beyond anything anyone could have ever imagined.

Spray painting his car was something she did for fun, but the Joy she was now would bypass a can of spray paint and issue a few slugs. Yes, when it came to Rell, she was prepared to catch a body, shaking as she held her cellphone in her hand.

If it's about Razz, suck some broken glass up your nose, homeboy. I'll never give up shit on my sister…BRO, she added in all capital letters, being petty.

"Got damn, Joy Joy going for blood. Old crazy ass," he said, chuckling as he headed to the bathroom in the airport. "I guess that's her way of saying she miss a nigga. Women," he said to himself before he responded to her text.

I'll holla, Joy Joy. Keep that same energy though. A nigga still love you for life, he texted back, looking around until he found the restroom. They had six hours before they had to be up and at their meeting, and Joy was being her usual self—stubborn and ignorant. Yet he still loved her.

Love, she texted back with a sad face. *Since when?*

That response alone made him think of the first time they'd met. It was at Piney Grove in the parking lot. She was being her loud and usual self when he walked by and didn't speak. Hating to be ignored, she called him out and he kept on walking until she chased him down. Four days later, he told her that he loved her and he meant it. He still did.

Love and miss us, too, Joy Joy. You know that. So I can't see you? I can slide through in two days. The locks haven't changed. My spot is your spot. Remember that.

Two days and not a day later, Rellon, she texted almost ten minutes later. *And no pussy.*

Girl, you were always more than pussy to me. And stop drinking, he texted her. Even if he weren't around her, he felt her. His bitch was drunk. *Love you, Joy Joy.*

I love you too, Rellon, she texted back, surprising him. He was always the more vocal one when it came to expressing anything outside of anger. He guessed time had softened her up a bit, and a bit was all he needed, sliding his cell back in his pocket.

After he took a leak, he washed his hands and headed out to the arrival area where Razz stood pouting and grumpy. In a matter of seconds, his mood had gone from being on a high, vibing with his Joy Joy, to dealing with Razz's bullshit and reckless behavior.

"Straight to the room, Razz. And no messing around when we check in. This meeting is important. Sis put in a lot of work for this, and we have that Bravo network meeting in two weeks if she's not back," he told him, patting him on the back. "Shake that shit off."

"Bruh, I know. See why I need her around?" he grumbled, dropping his head like a little boy in defeat. "She knows I can't act right whenever she forgets I need discipline," he pouted, serious as hell. "Why the hell she ain't come to Punta Cana, bro? For real?"

"And you wonder why she needs a break." Rell smiled, refusing to even co-sign or respond to his ignorant confession. Then it hit him why Razz had been successful—someone always had to keep him in line. Now that someone was him.

Chapter Thirteen

"Oh my, Denver. This is good, really good," Faith told him as she gushed, leaning down and slowly sipping the concoction he'd made. Each ingredient he added, he heard her hum or moan, smiling as she did. By the time he was done, he slid the drink her way as she sat on a bar stool, facing him. She pinched her lips before her tongue swiped the dribble easing out of her mouth.

Fuck, he thought, shaking his head. He wasn't sure how much longer he could take not touching her if she kept that up, walking around the bar to take a seat next to her.

"Glad you like it," he said, scooting closer against his better judgement.

"What's it called?" she finally asked, knowing that every drink had a name. He'd rattled off a few when they were in the kitchen area, but never mentioned the name of the one he'd made for her.

"I call it Sweet Carrotline. Like Carrot then line instead of Caroline."

"Caroline?" she asked with a lift of the brow, recognizing her middle name. She'd also tasted a hint of honey as she slowly sipped the carrot juice concoction. He actually slipped it in when she was checking her cell, wondering if she would taste it.

"Yeah, after you, Mouse," he said, bashfully as he tucked his lips in. "I have a few you inspired me to come up with actually."

"Yeah, right," she replied nervously, clearing her throat as she felt his hands against her lower back.

Fuck it. It's just a touch, he told himself while leaning closer to her.

"Why me?" she asked, sucking the straw tightly as she felt him kneading her back. Although she knew they were alone, she couldn't help wondering if the paparazzi had followed them there, especially after the little scene at the restaurant. While things had somewhat calmed down, she knew the tough part, the peeling of layers to figure out how they'd gotten to this point still needed to be discussed. But for now, she was indulging in this drink he'd named after her.

"Meaning?" he replied, wanting and needing to hear more.

"Why *still* think of me? I mean, I did sort of screw up my life, and it seems even yours too. Whoever did it definitely made sure I got the better end of the stick," she admitted, the guilt slowly overtaking her as she realized that Joy was right. She'd been played by her father and her husband, two men who were supposed to love and protect her and neither had.

She wouldn't say it out loud, but she knew in her heart that it had to be them. Besides, they were the only two who seemed to have move on with ease once he was gone. And somehow, without trying to, she'd learned to live without him. That was until now, feeling giddy as he looked at her.

"Why not you?" he asked her, inhaling her scent—that lemon and honey that made his nature rise. He was convinced she had to be born with it, since it was still there years later. He fought hard to ignore it, wishing he'd gotten some pussy the night before. Instead, he'd met up with his lawn team as he took a step back before heading to Mason from back home to handle business about his new business venture.

While his lawn service company was very successful, he wanted something that would allow him more down time. He knew a new business wouldn't do that right away, but it was in one place, and he planned to build a home in Mason if it really took off to stay permanently. He didn't hate Jonestown. He just couldn't live there anymore. Not when it represented a place of loss for him. "And you didn't do that shit all by yourself," he admitted, choosing his words carefully. "I could have fought harder, hunted your floppy ponytail ass down."

"I was not wearing ponytails then, you jerk," she said, laughing.

"You sure? This is a hairdo I've never seen you wear before," he said, with a pull that forced her body to rest against his. If she came over just a little more, she'd almost be on his lap.

"Just needed to get away," she said, her body feeling warm. She was unsure why he'd always labeled her as cool, when she felt sweat trickling down her breasts. Breasts that had grown, that rose and fell as she tried to adjust to their closeness.

"Yeah?" he replied just above a whisper, his hand softly squeezing her ass to which she smiled.

"Uh, yeah," she said, naturally looking around for any signs of paparazzi, even if they were alone in his juice bar.

"Without all the cameras, security, Razz…" she said, her voice trailing off as she looked over and studied his lips. Lips she wanted to taste as he swiped them once, taunting her.

"Whew," she released, and he laughed.

"Well, enough about that," he told her, smiling as she blushed and quickly looked away. He felt all giddy inside too, processing how quickly his life had changed in a matter of hours. Before church, he had never imagined ever seeing Faith again, let alone talking to her. Now he had her alone, wanting her too, and bad.

"Yes, enough about that," she released quietly when she looked his way again.

"Besides, we got time to make up for," he said, releasing her as he gave them some space. He thought he heard her suck her teeth, but he wasn't so sure.

"Wanna try something else?" he asked her, needing to find a way to get fucking Faith out of his head. Besides, she could never be just a fuck, and he didn't want her to be.

"I think I'll pass," she groaned, rubbing her stomach. "I'm so full," she whined with a playful pout when he slapped her ass. She yelped as he told her to shut up, rubbing her round, firm derriere. He might have given up the idea of sliding between her legs, but that didn't mean he was prepared to ignore all that ass she was carrying around.

"Fucking shame, Mouse. You gave that nigga my heart and my pussy," he whispered as he came up behind her, pulling a few tresses out of her face and over her shoulder. "The fuck you do that for?" he probed huskily. His nose then trailed up her neck then to her ear where he stopped. "One thousand four hundred and sixty days, Mouse," he released, his nose dragging up and down her ear, not expecting an answer to the question he'd posed about her giving herself to Razz.

"Of?" she dared to ask just above a whisper.

"Days away from you, ma," he confessed, his fingers grazing her shoulder when she tried to slide down off the bar stool. "Don't," he warned her, his voice low as he grabbed her hand. "Fuck with me for a little while. I was serious back there. I hope you were too. You owe a nigga that. Besides, a thunderstorm is coming, and guess where I need you to be?"

"Where?" she was scared to ask. *Please God, forgive me. I want him to say on his dick*, she thought, feeling the rub of his course index finger inside the palm of her hand as she closed her eyes.

"Where you should have always been. Where you are right now. Girl, the fuck with me. And tell Joy's ass to stop calling and texting," he demanded, slapping her ass once more as she stared at him in disbelief. "Don't even ask," was all he told her, allowing her to ease off the stool before they heard a series of taps at the door.

Chapter Fourteen

"Knight Commodore has a girlfriend," Denver stated the obvious once they were alone. "That's crazy. Queen actually allowed someone to sit on the throne in the Commodore palace," he teased.

"Man, Queen don't run shit," Knight lied, smiling because until Noel showed up, Queen did just that. She ran everyone and everything—him, his brother, their entire company.

"Hey, Queen!" Denver shouted out with a wave of the hand, causing Knight to jump as he looked in that direction. "I thought Queen don't run shit?"

"Shut up," Knight grumbled as they took a walk through downtown Mason. They were headed back to the juice bar after dropping the ladies off to a boutique store for Faith to pick up a few things. She'd already changed her hair, but she was feeling lighter and in a much better mood, when Noel suggested they visit a place she'd fallen in love with. Both men were surprised the girls hit it off so soon, but it also meant they weren't stuck having to go shopping, something they both would have dreaded.

After Faith and Denver fought like an old married couple about her not checking into a hotel and, instead, crashing with him, she'd calmed down long enough to be introduced to Noel. Noel immediately took to her, happy she had some female company to hang out with. Something that was rare outside of spending time with her sister, Nyla, who was married with two children.

"This better impress me, or I'm leaving nasty ass reviews on Yelp as soon as this bitch open," he told his childhood friend with a playful scowl on his face.

"I'm not worried about that. Like you have Queen, I have Brianna, and she stays on her shit," he told him as they approached the street his juice bar was on.

They parked a few blocks away, wanting to catch up as they took in a few sights in Mason. That magic Knight always felt was still in the air, inhaling as he looked around. He was glad his friend was there too after the life they lived growing up.

"I could live here permanently, you know," he admitted to Knight, enjoying the calm energy and smiles on people's faces as they spoke and waved. "No rush, not all the city noise and low crime rate."

"Hell, practically none. Generations of business owners and families are raising their children in Mason. They believe in what they've created, supported, and they don't mind looking out for each other," he said, thinking of the Bookers, an older couple who owned the grocery store in town. They loved Noel and Knight and were the reason the two of them had met over the holidays the year before. So each time he and Noel came to Mason, a stop at the Bookers was a must.

"It's why you purchased a few properties out here?"

"Queen's idea to visit here led to that, to be honest. She wanted us to spend more time as a family away from work. Then King came up with the purchasing part. We came out here over Christmas since Mason's a nice spot for tourists, and the rest is history. We have four cabins out here we rent out like timeshares, but Noel loves this place. It's why we're here. She wants to open up a pet store."

"Knight has himself an entrepreneur," Denver said, smiling. "I can see how that interests you, a woman that wants her own."

"Honestly, Noel would have been stuck working for her parents and married to her so-called best friend if I didn't stop that shit. Dude's a lame that was dragging my baby. Anyway, enough about my love life. What's up with Mouse?" he probed, adding a chuckle. "You know I know that woman's name is not Mouse. I recognize Faith's ass. I don't give a fuck how much weight she's put on or how she wears her hair. Hell, I'm like you. I pay attention to detail. She was all nervous and shit, squirming when I repeated her name. Now Noel's a little naïve, but shit, she's getting better."

"Her name is Mouse," Denver countered, smiling since only her family and Razz knew he called her that.

"Anyway," he told him, dismissing what he was talking about. "Do what you feel is right, but while you're doing it, tell me the real reason why she's here in fucking Mason, hundreds of miles away from her husband or wherever the hell he is?"

"Check the blogs, nigga," Denver scoffed. "Then asked what *he* did. Her ass still hasn't told me what's up. But you know I stay investigating. Shorty ain't just leave the celebrity life to chill in a small ass town. But like always, Mouse rather live a lie than live in her truth. I ain't pushing it if she don't want to talk about it. And honestly, I don't give a fuck."

"Not a lie, D. Truth is you didn't really give her much choice if she did leave your ass in prison. You never leveled with her before all that shit with Solo went down. I knew something would come back to bite our ass that day. I swear I did," he told him.

After scrolling through a few social media blog sites, Knight fell out laughing. He knew Amber very well. Had fucked her a few times, too, since Commodore Enterprises opened up a lot of doors for him and that meant doors that came with a gang of women, too.

"Damn, Razz's moving like that?" Knight said, putting his cellphone away.

"Yeah, like that. Fucking clown," Denver replied, slamming two glasses on the counter. "I need a drink," he said, causing Knight to laugh.

"Naw, what you need is to remember how far you've come. I thought you told me you were saved, all back in church," he probed, watching Denver unravel as he closed his eyes, rolling his neck around.

"I'm good," he lied. "Me and God are good too."

"But are you happy? How's the baby? Kay's straight?" Knight probed even more, referring to his goddaughter.

"Hell yeah," he lied again, refusing to tell him about Dashon. He'd warned him too about her friendly pussy, confident she had fucked more inmates than him, but Denver just couldn't resist how easily she gave it up.

"So you and the baby mama are *really* good," he fished, looking at him in his eyes.

"Good if co-parenting counts… when she lets it." He

laughed. "And that is rare, you feel me?" he said, dropping his head as he slid his hand down his waves.

"Hell naw, I don't feel you. It's why I don't have kids, but with Noel… shit, as soon as she lets me fill her up with babies, bruh, it's on," he told him, looking around as if she were nearby. "She stay asking me to give her, her pills so I know she's not trying to trap me. Fuck that. It's me that wants to trap her ass," he admitted, causing them both to release a hearty laugh.

"Damn, life must be good with her," Denver said, nodding his head.

"Damn good with her," he admitted, getting emotional. He didn't have the love of a mother or knew how to properly love a woman. But with Noel, he was learning every day, and she was patient with him as he did. She was his confidant, his best friend, and he'd spend every day proving to her that she was worth whatever he'd learn he needed to give her and more. "Can't just keep sticking dick to these bitches, D."

"Bruh, you know me. I was doing a little something to pass the time, and she turned out to be a cool girl, and a nigga was caged in around a bunch of dicks. The fuck I look like turning down pussy and free pussy? Then I figured it was fate when I picked up a few contracts in this new part of town after I got out. Never knew one of those contracts would be with her ass." He laughed. He had to since it seemed like God most times really just hated him, as he sat there feeling anxious, wondering if Faith would take off once out of his sight. He looked out the glass window a few times and sat up, catching Knight's attention.

"Yo, Noel's probably talking her ear off, especially if she caught on to who she is. I swear my girl's a blondie sometimes, but blondie or not, I'll fucking kill for that one," he said, nodding his head.

Denver admired how smitten Knight was when it came to Noel. He'd go broke to get her and her family anything they wanted. The pet store he was opening up for her wasn't even a dent in his pocket. The construction had just started, and he spared no expense. Every time she turned around, he was asking her what she needed when all he wanted from her in return was her hand in marriage. Things were still new, though. Still, that didn't mean marriage wasn't right for them if he had to tell it.

"Word?"

"Fuck yeah," he spat.

"Yo, you're crazy for real," Denver said, slapping his boy's shoulder as he broke a smile.

"So uh, you sure you don't want to crash at the cabin? Bad weather's coming our way, and I don't think you two need to be cooped up alone for that," he told him, hoping his friend was thinking clearly with his head.

They hadn't had a chance to spend much time alone since Denver had been released short of his homecoming party and a few community events Denver pitched in to help with. Since Knight's company owned a hospital now, it was a no-brainer when Denver secured the commercial landscaping contract and a few others tied to Knight's businesses. They'd promised each other a long time ago that once poverty was no longer their lot, they'd forever find ways to make money together, and they were off to a good start.

"I heard, but you know I finally got me a spot here with three bedrooms. Renting for now, but she can park in one of those rooms. I'm not trying to fuck, bruh. I'm serious. Just trying to see where we went wrong, you feel me? Talk shit out."

"I feel you, D," he said before he took a deep breath to ask him the next real issue. "Told her about Kay?"

If anyone knew the havoc that came behind Denver refusing to marry Dashon before she announced her pregnancy, Knight did. Since then, he hadn't found anyone else close to making him want to settle down. Someone that would ever fill that space, that hole that only Faith could fill. Unlike Faith, he decided he would never marry anyone he couldn't see forever with, and he and Dashon had been feuding ever since.

"I haven't yet," he admitted, sighing. "Shit just didn't come up," he told him, not sure if he would have, even if there was a space for him to share. A safe space. that is. Faith was already fragile, and way before her failed marriage became a public failed one.

"Omission is just the same as a lie. Clean it up, D. Clean it up," his friend warned him.

"I'm trying," he replied, feeling a tightness in his chest. He loved his daughter unconditionally, the same way he loved Faith. His biggest fear now was having to choose—something he prayed he'd never have to do, even if Faith was only back in his life as a friend.

"Don't try. Just tell her. The Faith I know couldn't hold it against you. Seven years, D. A lot has happened in seven years, and one is you having a child. Don't make it seven more or longer. Not when divorce is looking pretty good if those blogs had to tell it and from the way she was looking at you."

"She was checking your boy out, huh?" Denver replied cockily, grinning.

"Whatever. Just handle your business before you fuck up

my time here. I can hear it now, Noel having a new bestie she's ready to defend. Women are a trip. I'm telling you. They're probably all on your page now, screenshotting and shit," he said, causing Denver to quickly whip out his cell.

"See." Knight laughed. "Don't change your privacy settings, nigga. Just live right, and the rest of what you got going on will follow."

"Fuck you," Denver growled. "Imagine you being the relationship expert."

"I'm not. Just a nigga in love and one who plans to stay that way," Knight told him, shooting Noel a text. He never missed a chance to let her know she was on his mind, and already, he was missing her.

Chapter Fifteen

"I thought we were going to the boutique?" Faith probed. After getting dropped off by the men since Knight wanted to possibly invest in the bar, the girls decided they could get a little shopping in since Faith needed a few things. Once they did, Noel dragged her a few stores down as they stood in front of an adult novelty and lingerie shop.

"I am, but this is shopping too," Noel informed her, shooting her mischievous smile that made Faith snicker. In fact, that's all she'd been doing since she'd met Noel. The ice was broken shortly after introductions when Noel complimented her on her hair. Faith wasn't sure if she recognized her or not, but since she didn't say anything, she figured she was in the clear.

"Oh, I see," Faith replied, as they entered. The store, Fancy's, was a combination of a Victoria's Secret meets Adam and Eve, an adult novelty shop.

Early on in her marriage, she attempted to add lingerie to her wardrobe at the advice of her sisters due to her inexperience. She soon learned, however, that Razz could care less about lingerie or foreplay. Sex was methodical—a kiss here and groan there and then one push before he was inside of her.

"Knight wouldn't care if I wore a big t-shirt with a big hole in it to bed, but I won't lie. He really turns it up when I add a little satin and lace," she whispered and giggled. Noel had gone from a clueless yet beautiful tomboy to a woman in touch with her femininity.

Between her sister and her brother Neil's girlfriend, Cassidy, Noel's tomboy phase experienced a rapid death. She still enjoyed the flexibility of her casual attire which consisted of jeans, tanks, and boy shorts, but with a man like Knight Commodore, she was eager to release her feminine side. Knight never pressured her, but Noel couldn't resist seeing how his eyes lit up each time she wore something that accentuated her petite yet shapely figure.

"You sure you want company tonight?" Faith asked, scratching the back of her neck. Just because her love life had gone to hell didn't mean she wanted to impose because Noel had embraced her. It did, however, give her time to possibly get out of the arrangement she'd made with Denver. She could barely sit still around him fully clothed, so being alone with him all day and night and for days would be a struggle. That and the fact that she remained married. "We really can just skip it and connect another day."

"I mean, unless you have someplace you'd rather be," she replied, nudging her in the arm. "I can even help you pick out a few things."

"Oh, no. You mean with Denver? Girl, pfft," she said, shaking her head. "Denver and I are not together like that. Just friends." She laughed nervously. "Old friends, like what? Many, many years ago," she exaggerated.

"Who said anything in here was for Denver?" Noel probed nosily, hoping she'd get her to speak on what was really going on with Knight's old friend who was definitely eye candy and single.

"Oh, right," she said, attempting to recover. "To be honest, I'm not exactly in a happy place when it comes to dating, love—any of that stuff. In fact, love and I are not even on the same page, let alone in the same book."

"Well, coming to Mason just might be exactly what you needed. Ever heard of what they say about Mason?" Noel asked her excitedly.

"That it's small?" Faith replied, still surprised no one had recognized her, yet grateful.

"That too, but no. It's the place of magic and love. A place where things not only happen *to* you but *for you.* That's the beauty of it. But the smallness makes it intimate and personal. No one is a stranger, and even if they are, they won't be for long—like us. And that, my dear, is where the magic starts. As for love, you're on your own," she teased while Faith smiled, shaking her head.

"Not interested in love, but yeah, you're cool," Faith told her, lightly bumping her shoulder as they walked up the aisle slowly, looking around.

"Oh, and another thing I forgot to mention," she sang, stopping and facing her new friend.

Damn, she knows, she thought to herself as Noel leaned in, lessening the space in between them.

"It's also where Knight and I met and fell in love," she said instead when Faith exhaled.

Whew! That was close, very close, she thought to herself, smiling as Noel's eyes lit up when she did.

"That is dope, Noel. Aww," she cooed as she gave her a half hug.

"And where it could happen for you. Girl, I saw how Denver was looking at you. He's a goner for you, Mouse. Why you two are pretending, beats me."

"I doubt he is," she said, sliding a few lingerie pieces on the rack in front of her. She had no interest in buying anything, but any talk about Denver and love would surely trip her up. "But congrats on finding love here, girl. Trust me, I'm okay."

"Oh well. It still doesn't hurt to look around and pick up an outfit or two. Just don't overthink it. Then I can cook before my lingerie and liquor time with my man tonight," she told Faith whose mouth dropped.

"Oh, I like that," Faith softly squealed, clapping her hands.

"Oh the things that happen during lingerie and liquor night," Noel told her, slipping her arm through Faith's. "Come on, let's check out that rack over there. Then we can head to the boutique."

"Yes, the boutique." She was ready to get out of there and fast.

"What do you think about this?" Noel asked her, handing her a black laced lingerie nighty that cupped the breast area tightly. It flowed down with ease just below the hips with a huge slit in the front. It was playful and sexy at the same time.

"No," she said immediately. "Uh un. Nope, nope, nope." She could barely think straight, wondering not only how she would look in it, but what would happen if she wore it. That was still farfetched, but it screamed Pornhub very loudly with the open crotch and low-cut breast area.

"Why not? If it's not for Denver, buy it for whoever it is

that you would wear it for at some point in your life," Noel suggested.

"Ugh," Faith said, giving up as she took it from her and pressed it against her body in a nearby mirror. "I do kind of like it," she said more so to herself.

"Me too," Noel chimed in. "Now all you have to do is get it."

"Sheesh, what am I doing?" she groaned, as Noel took it out of her hand.

"Buying this lingerie and maybe even one more, *Faith Streeter*," she added as Faith gasped, looking around.

"Wait—"

"Girl, your secret is safe with me," she whispered, smiling as she girl fanned over the celebrity. "I knew you looked familiar, but that name Mouse just wasn't convincing. Sorry, Faith," she told her, poking out her bottom lip. "You forgive me? Trust me, I'm not a stalker, but you're beautiful. Too beautiful to hide that beauty, no matter what those blogs are saying," she informed her, after quickly checking the internet to see why Faith Streeter was even in Mason. Celebrities didn't come there that often, but when they did, Mason and all its residents knew.

"I don't even want to know."

"Ridiculous shit, girl. Heck, I might need to call up my brother, Neil. He'll kick your husband's cheating ass," she told her, causing Faith to bust out in a fit of laughter.

"Are we related?" she asked in between laughs, covering her mouth.

"We can be. Just let me know. Neil still ain't fond of Knight. One call and he'll drive up here in a hurricane to prove to Knight that he don't play about me."

"Neil, you said?" she repeated, a devilish grin appearing on her face.

"Shit, well I guess I don't play about Mouse then either," they both heard Denver whisper behind Faith's ear, causing her to yelp. "The fuck you asking about Neil for, Mouse? That list of niggas keep getting longer, I see," he told her, holding her firmly around her waist.

"Denver," she said with a tight smile before Noel grabbed another lingerie off the rack, fighting hard not to smile.

"We'll take both of these," Noel called out to the associate as Denver nipped on Faith's ear with his teeth.

"That's for me, shorty?" he asked her. Faith felt her center pulsate from the closeness and the feel of his stubble against her face. It was just like old times, the playful energy instantly returning coupled with that sexual chemistry.

"Move," she told him as he started tickling her. "Stop it!" she squealed. "I didn't mean anything by it. I was just confirming his name. I'm not playing with you today, Den."

"Good," he told her, nipping her ear again. "Because I was *never* playing about you. Now pick out a few more things, shorty. Hurry up," he told her, meaning it.

"What?" she asked, leaning back and smiling at him. "For what?"

"For us, Mouse. One day, we *will* use them," he assured her with confidence. "Now stop looking at me like you're ready to gobble a nigga up. I'm celibate with your nasty ass," he teased, when a huge smile stretched across her face.

"For how long?" she replied, playing along when he turned her around and squatted, resting his lips against hers.

"I can come out of retirement right fucking now," he whispered, before kissing her slowly and sensually, tossing caution to the wind.

"I told you, girl," Noel called out to them. Once Faith leaped into his arms, a few photos were clicked, and within hours, she and Razz Streeter were trending yet again from *Twitter* to *Instagram* to *TMZ*.

Photos that sold for thirty grand at the expense of Faith's momentary hideout.

Chapter Sixteen

"Razz was really selling drugs?" Faith asked as they lay in the dark. After hours of eating, drinking, and finally kicking it without all the tension, the rest of the day ended on a high note. They hadn't brought up the letter, and before Faith knew it, she was in the room she'd accepted as a place to crash instead of the hotel. The only issue was Denver followed her in that room.

"Why the fuck you think he got arrested?"

"Your mouth," she huffed, shaking her head.

"Aye, I'm not the preacher or gospel singer," he told her, laughing. "Your daddy and husband are."

"Soon to be ex-husband, thank you very much, and Daddy's mouth is not filthy."

No, but that bitch's hands are, Denver thought to himself, pulling Faith over to his side of the bed.

"Look," he said, fighting to keep his eyes opened. "Marriage requires daily renewal, Mouse. What have you done to renew it, to repair it? I mean, I'd rather your ass get a divorce, but I'm no rebound nigga. This is the friend in me rapping with you. Not the nigga that loves you," he told her honestly. That and he was testing her too. If she bailed on him and then on Razz and then him again, she wasn't a victim. That's just who she was when things became rough and complicated.

"Have you been listening to anything I've been saying, Denver?" she asked him, trying to sit up, but he wouldn't let her. "No, I'm serious. I didn't want to marry Razz in the first place, so this cheating scandal was just another reason why I shouldn't have married him." She stopped short of telling him it wasn't Razz's first time, since telling him that made her look weak. She already felt weak, so no way was she giving him more ammunition to make her feel any worse than she already did.

"And again, I didn't write the damn letter telling you that we were over. Shit!" she released, wrestling with him to get out of the bed.

"Whoa." He chuckled, pulling on her wrists. "But it's me with a dirty mouth? And lay your ass back, Mouse. It was a question. You know me. As soon as you get to crying, everything after that is out the door for me. I'm wired like that about you. Always have been," he said, forcing her to lay underneath his arm as he threw his legs over her body. "Now lay the fuck down," he said softly in her ear, smiling as she grunted.

He couldn't help but laugh, watching her face all scrunched up as he pinched her nose.

"And chill out with that anyway. You're too pretty to have a dirty mouth."

"You're too pretty to have a dirty mouth," she repeated, mimicking him. "That's all you have to say? I'm telling you that I don't want him, and—" she fussed before his lips came crashing against hers.

Their tongues danced around each other as Denver rose up, pushing her flat on her back before he rested between her legs. The kiss grew even more intense once he gripped her neck, slightly choking her. Her mouth opened as a light hiss escaped, causing Denver's hand to slip in between her legs. Her pussy was wet and warm, leaking through her satin panties.

"Fuck me," she whispered, her eyes studying his as her chest heaved up and down. She'd been wanting to feel his length and girth all day that did a poor job of hiding. The curve alone made her come just watching him as she found a restroom to clean up before they left the adult novelty shop the minute he rested her center against it. It was sinless, so sinless but she wanted him and right then. "Fuck me, please."

He wanted to but things were fresh, too fresh and he'd have to kill Faith for playing with his heart this time around, no matter what she'd told him earlier.

"Shorty, you don't even know what you want," he whispered against her mouth, despite pulling and sucking her bottom lip. "And what I told you about your mouth, cursing and shit. That's not my Mouse," he whispered, slowly working her center with two fingers as her legs fell to each side. "Pussy so wet," he groaned, pecking her lips one time.

Her back arched, causing Denver's head to rest in between her breasts. His strong, muscular arms wrapped around her, lifting her off the bed. For the first time since she'd had sex, Faith felt desired and alive. When she got a grunt followed by a series of unintelligible responses, she felt beyond sexy, beyond desired.

She felt like *his*.

Then he stopped quickly, pulling back as she squirmed and reached for him, in shock. He knew everything there was to know about a woman, from the feel of her breasts, how to caress them and how to suck on her nipples until they peaked with joy. From the different designs of her lower lips that bloomed and swelled as blood rushed to the surface, causing a woman's nerve endings to go in a frenzy around her clitoris.

Faith was crying, panting, begging him to finish when he asked, "Have you ever had your pussy ate, Mouse? Or ever had an orgasm?"

When he did, a scowl formed on his face when she covered hers and turned to her side.

"Mouse, baby, I'm not trying to upset or embarrass you," he told her, pulling on her hands so she could face him, her eyes still tightly shut. "I'm saying though," he continued, pulling her toward him. "Has he ever even made love to you, where you got off, you got your shit and came? Where it was all about you?"

Peeking as she opened one eye, she whispered, "No. No, he hasn't."

"That motherfucker," he groaned, resting back on his haunches.

Chapter Seventeen

Once he took his time, washing and cleaning Faith up, he gave her a t-shirt and demanded she get back in bed. While he wanted to ask her why she didn't demand more or want more from a man, especially when it came to pleasing her, the answer was simple—Faith was still that girl he'd loved seven years ago. A girl that wanted to experience everything with him and he with her yet had settled. A girl that didn't even know how to ask for what she wanted from a man. A girl that took a leap in the moment and asked him, yet he'd politely declined. Instead he sucked on her pussy for two hours until she released and cried and cried and released, then he told her that the day she was divorced, he'd planned to fuck her to sleep, and she smiled.

As the rain began to pick up, since it seemed sleep was nowhere in sight, he asked her again about the letter. The one she supposedly hadn't written.

"I think I know who wrote it," she confessed, fear settling

in. She never wanted to see this person in this light, but things were starting to become clearer and clearer to her the more she and Denver went down memory lane since their paths had crossed.

Rushing out the door for rehearsal, Faith grabbed her bookbag that rested by the bedroom door. She wanted to get in and out so she could spend a little time with Razz. Things had been going well despite their rocky start, and while she was devastated behind Denver removing her off of his visitation list, she'd accepted that maybe it was for the best.

They'd done more than six shows after the youth summer jam, and their music was being played on local radio shows. Overnight, everyone began to see them as a budding young couple who shared their love for the gospel, ministering through the gift of music. Joy wasn't too fond of Razz anymore, eyeing him every time he showed up while Mercy praised him.

"You look beautiful," Razz told her as she slid into his car, smiling bashfully. They hadn't done much besides hold hands, but it was clear the attraction was now mutual. Her father even encouraged it, often calling them out in service to perform impromptu which sometimes meant a sermon wasn't even preached. The spirit sometimes would get so high from praise and worship, all there was time for was for the offering plates to be passed and a quiet benediction.

"This thing," she said, staring down at her khaki dress. "Joy picked it out," she revealed, actually appreciating her sister's fashion taste.

She'd never allow her to go overboard, but she had to admit that Joy really had an eye for fashion. Underneath, she wore a soft yellow tube top that complemented her smooth mocha-colored skin. Her yellow sandals revealed toes that wiggled, proving she was nervous. Razz, like Denver, noticed Faith's feet were the most sensitive part of her body. Even when she played or wrote music, she kept time with one foot while the lyrics and melody danced around in her head.

"Joy's crazy butt," he chided, shaking his head. He knew she had a crush on him or used to, often ignoring her, which didn't go unnoticed. He

figured why wait a few years for the sister when he could have Faith right then. That and the fact he'd misjudged Faith. She really was a woman he saw himself being with, loving and even marrying.

"Hmph, tell me about it," she said, digging in her bookbag. "Wait, let me make sure I have my songbook," she told him, pulling out Mercy's diary instead. "Oh wow, I don't… Gimme a sec. Good thing I looked," she said before she got out and headed inside. Once she made it into their bedroom, she tripped on one of Mercy's shoes, causing the diary to fall out and flip over.

She never once thought it was appropriate to read anyone's innermost thoughts, but she couldn't help it when she saw Denver's name in bold letters followed by a heart. She stretched her eyes a few times, wondering if it were a joke, but when she heard her mother calling her from the living room, she closed it and placed it aside. Weeks later, she noticed Mercy would throw up Denver's name here or there, especially whenever Razz was on his way. She even tried to make her feel bad for so called moving on.

"Mercy was feeling me?" he asked, laughing but not out of humor. "Mouse, everyone knew Mercy was into Knight. Why would she even be thinking about me and enough to do some shit like that?" he asked, sitting up in disbelief. Disbelief and hurt, so hurt he was starting to question his own judgement, staring at Faith suspiciously.

"So you still don't believe me? Wow." She laughed when his cell phone started ringing. "Might as well get that. Anyone calling you at midnight clearly has a reason to. Yet I'm the one who's lying," she said, getting up.

"Mouse, come on now. This entire day has been fucking with me. Chill. Always trying to run. The fuck you going in the rain anyway?" he fussed, leaning over and seeing it was Dashon. "Fucking great. I got to take this," he regretfully informed her, getting up and walking out of the room. Especially when she never called him this late.

He didn't have to see Faith's face. He already knew she was hurt and heard it too when she threw something at the door before he closed it.

Chapter Eighteen

"A daughter," Faith whispered when he eased back into the room. She couldn't help but eavesdrop, her heart being ripped from her body when she heard him say it.

"Where is she now? Your daughter, I mean?" she asked, unsure how she felt if she and her mother lived with him. She was so naïve, so green when it came to men. She was starting to wonder if anything they'd experienced over the years between them was real.

"With her mother, but I get her every other week or weekend, just depends on our schedule," he said, quickly filling in the blanks without shitting on his daughter's mother. She was somewhat relieved but not enough since the mere fact he had a daughter was still a factor. "Shorty, we're just coparenting," he added, as if he heard her thoughts. "That's it, Mouse. I swear."

"I didn't think otherwise nor did I ask," she lied, just not out loud.

"You didn't have to. That's what two people do in a relationship. They talk, they communicate."

"Well, we are not in a relationship. I was just asking since it's pretty late at night or early in the morning. You know what I mean," she said, fighting hard not to have an attitude as she gave him her back. She was tired of crying, refusing to do it over something she could never change.

"Apparently someone saw us earlier. Baby mama told me," he informed her, sighing as he scooted up behind her and pulled her body into his. "Check the net, Mouse," he told her, kissing her on her cheek. "And stop fucking pouting. I said coparenting, Mouse," he reemphasized, detecting her attitude as her body stiffened.

"I hear you, and I'll pass. Used to it," she said, sniffling. "I guess she's pretty pissed."

"Fuck that girl. She don't know you, and you don't know her. And to be honest, you're blessed not to. If it weren't for my daughter, I wouldn't give a damn about what she thinks or feels. I still don't, keeping that shit real. I just don't want people shitting on your name, ma. Trust me, I know how that feels," he told her, kissing her shoulder which caused her body to rest against his.

"Like what? The shitting on my name part?" she asked, curious as she turned to face him. She smiled as the dimly lit moon allowed her to see his face. He was still beautiful to her, lazy brown eyes and lips that curled just a little when he smiled back. Still, she could see he was tired and frustrated yet kept smiling when he looked into her eyes.

"Shorty just mad because I'm not fucking with her like that. She went on and on about us being all over *The Shade Room* and *TMZ*. Said they're calling you the 'whoring pastor's daughter that would and did' like what your husband did was justified. The fuck out of here. Then accused me of sleeping with a married woman."

"We didn't though," she said, although she wished they had, still feeling the stubble of hair that lightly bruised her inner thigh area. Her center jumped too when he kissed her again, this time under her ear.

"I ate that sweet ass pussy though." He laughed as she covered her face, smiling. She never knew one person could ever make another one feel that good, so alive. She was close to asking him if he could do it again before he told her to chill when she pulled his hand between her legs.

"Well, for what it's worth. I'm sorry I pulled you into all of this," she told him, tucking her lips as she felt her pussy jump once more. She wasn't sure if all women experienced this, but if they got together and were married, she was sure she'd be pregnant in no time.

"Naw, ma. Fuck that. It's not all on you."

"I'm for real and I'm too coward to look, I guess. Especially if you saw the other stuff… about Razz," she admitted. "Did you see that too?"

"Yeah." He sighed, pulling her into his chest where she rested her head. "The ones with Razz and the chick, Amber and a few of us. Fucking lies. Just crazy." Sadly, once the pictures were leaked, Razz went from being the slimy, ungrateful husband to one that was forced to seek love and affection elsewhere. The narrative soon flipped, and now he had somehow became the victim.

Still, Denver found the pictures of him and her endearing as he watched how cute she looked in his arms. She looked happy, light, and in love.

"Look, for what it's worth, I'm happy for you. Having a

child must be a wonderful thing," she said, tracing the tattoo across his chest.

"My daughter's name," he whispered, close to showing her another one that was on the other side. He didn't, figuring it would only make her feel worse, so he'd let it go. "Kasia Ann Daniels."

"Ann's her middle name?"

"Naw, no middle name. I told her she wasn't about to confuse my fucking kid with fourteen names. Black people be doing the most." He laughed. "Her grandmother. She named her after her," he told her. "They were close, and she died while Dashon was pregnant," he said as Faith took note of her name.

"Yeah, gone 'head and tell Noel her name," he said, smiling. "I already know how you women operate, creating fake pages and stalking. I'm fucked." He laughed, when they heard a large boom sound, knocking the power out.

"Oh my God," she screamed, pushing herself even further underneath him.

"Scary ass. No more hanging out with Noel. I see you not being around your gangster sisters is starting to affect you. By now, the three of you would have beat my ass," he teased, shifting as he adjusted his body so she could get comfortable. "We might as well accept that we'll be together for a few days," he told her, glad the topic of his daughter was out in the open. "Food in the fridge is cold, but I'll hook up the generator later. Nigga tired. All that pussy eating wore me out."

"Be quiet," she spat, playfully poking him in the chest.

"It was, and a nigga full. Fuck that food in the fridge," he added, getting comfortable himself when Faith sat up. "Damn, Mouse. What now?"

"You know I think I should call my mother. By now, she's

worried and… she's kind of blocked," she admitted, unsure how many days they'd be under bad weather. They'd spoken only once since she landed in Jonestown, and after her mother fussed about her not coming home where they lived, she hung up and put her on the block list.

"What the hell, Mouse?" he fussed, looking at her like she was crazy. "Girl, you better call your mother. Tell her I said what's up, too. Besides, you can't hide forever, Mouse. That nigga got to know that even if it's not me, it can't be him. I'll kill him before I let you go back, shorty," he told her, issuing a threat he had every intention on keeping.

Chapter Nineteen

"Damn, who is that?" Theodore asked his best friend, Shakur, whose name was the reason they'd become best friends.

Theodore, a known clown that received clout solely from being a Valentine, went in hard the day he was introduced to his peers in Sunday school. In no time at all, a brawl ensued when Theodore asked him how he was a Christian when he seemed to proudly carry a Muslim name. He found out that day that not only did he have a Muslim name, but he also had Muslim hands like the great Muhammed Ali.

Soon, the popular, good looking Jonestown guy all the girls swooned over woke up minutes later with a black eye and literally short term memory, and their punishment was community hours with the Senior Saint ministry for a month. A month after being around a gang of old ladies led them to being best friends. Shortly after that, a new girl in town showed up —Valerie Carmichael.

"Who?" Shakur replied, not even looking up as they waited for Sunday School to start. Shakur hadn't even prepared for their Sunday School lesson but had to or fear the wrath of Sister Gilbert. She was like the bible thumping grim reaper of Piney Grove. The last thing he wanted

was to have to spend a second later in a classroom with her. She reeked of moth balls, and if asked, she had hands that did more touching on his shoulder and back then they did the Bible.

"This bitch right here," he mumbled, catching Shakur's attention when he heard the word "bitch". Rarely did any girl have Theodore's attention or interest that long, and if he called them out of their name, chances are, they had history. A history that had rubbed Theodore the wrong way. Still, when it came to knowledge about the Bible, Theodore was at the top in Sunday school. Well, that was after Shakur had been slacking, keeping up with Theodore and the many girls that made it almost too easy for him to have his way with them.

When he saw no one that could elicit that response from his friend, he looked around as he sat up slightly. His forehead creased from confusion.

"Her, Sha. Dang, pay attention," he told him, roughly nudging his arm which caused his Bible to fall on the floor.

"Dang, man is right. It's not that serious," Shakur grumbled, leaning down to pick it up. "I'm already tired, and Sister Gilbert gave us the look this morning during early morning worship. I could barely keep my eyes open."

"Yeah, whatever. That bitch is fine. That's a whole lot of ass and the prettiest smile to keep any guy alert," he told Shakur, casually speaking inappropriately as if they weren't in church like he always did. "Even you have to admit that. I don't know why you keep pretending like all of this is interesting to you," he said, referring to them being prepared to go into ministry.

For Theodore, the path had been laid out for him since his grandfather and father were already pastors at Piney Grove Ministries, but for Shakur, it was a choice. While he may have had a Muslim name, it was given to him by a father who'd abandoned him and his mother when Shakur was just two years old. It wasn't until almost middle school did he realize he had a name deemed Muslim, but by that time, he'd accepted it whether he liked it or not. What he loved more was the gospel and how it had changed his mother's life and ultimately his.

"Here she comes," he said quickly, sitting up while Shakur's body stiffened from her smell alone. It was a soft lemon one, one that smelled beyond expensive but a girl their age would never wear. It even lingered as she stood, looking around to find a place to sit.

"'Sup, what's your name?" Theodore probed coolly although Shakur watched her tapping her right foot. He chuckled, wondering how a girl that Theodore had just lay eyes on would have unnerved him without saying a word. Sure, she smelled good, but Shakur, even though intrigued by her smell and looks, felt a girl needed more than that to unnerve him. Even at fifteen since he'd secretly realized he preferred more mature girls. The ones who didn't play games and were certain about what they wanted from a guy and even better, life.

"Sup?" she repeated with a frown. "Eww, who speaks like that? Is that even English?" she probed, chuckling with a look of disgust on her face. "No, thank you," she replied, making her way past them as a few of the youth nearby laughed.

Shakur couldn't help but snicker as well, casting a glance over his shoulder at the young beauty's way. With skin the color of lightly creamed coffee coupled with high cheekbones and slanted eyes, Shakur unconsciously held his breath until she was no longer in his sight as she got up and moved once more.

"Fuck her," Theodore mumbled, looking over his shoulder, which seemed to happen without him even trying to. "She must be new to Jonestown. Has to be, but it's cool. By the end of the summer, I'll have her pent up in the church closet, or on her knees in the bathroom. I don't know. If' she's a virgin, I might want to keep her like that until I marry her."

"Marry her?" Shakur spat louder than he'd intended.

"Bro, chill," he warned him with a scowl. "I'm just saying. I'm expected to take over this church. I've had just about every girl here already

in some way. I have to save at least one that my grandfather and father would approve of. I'm running out of options, then here she comes. Might be fate."

"She has to want you back first, bro," Shakur told him, silently praying she'd maintain that same posture. Without even knowing her, Shakur could tell there was something special about her. But like always, Theodore's charm and quick wit not only got him the girl but the wife that was supposed to be Shakur's.

"Sir," Deacon Reuben said through the door, lightly tapping on it. They'd been on the road most of the week after Sunday's service, and the deacon was ready to head back home. Pastor Valentine had a packed house each night, celebrating the twentieth pastoral anniversary of one of his closest friends, Apostle White. Like Pastor Valentine, he too had one of the largest congregations in Tuckerville, a city up north. Deacon Monroe stopped traveling with him long ago, initially because of his wife, Melvina, who fell ill and passed away from cancer. Once she did, he just couldn't stomach the blatant disregard his best friend had for First Lady Valerie, so he stopped going altogether.

"Pastor," Deacon Rueben whispered roughly, tapping on the door even harder. They had less than one hour to get to Tuckerville International Airport.

"I must go now," Pastor Theodore said to the mocha-colored beauty, tracing his finger down her thick thigh. It was no secret to his wife that her husband had a thing for darker-skinned women, especially since she was quite fair-skinned.

She had overlooked it like she did many times whenever his eyes wandered to women of that complexion, but her patience had grown thin after learning about Razz's indiscretions. It was like history repeating itself even more. "When I land—"

"Theo, please don't. It was fun. I did what you needed me to do... like always," she said and laughed. She pulled and wrapped the sheet around her body, giving him a glance over her shoulder.

For fifty-nine, Pastor Theodore Valentine easily attracted women from all ages, but he could go further with the younger ones. Legal yet still younger. They didn't ask too many questions, and they did whatever he wanted them to do. In return, a trinket here, a ticket to fly out to wherever he was, was enough, and he preferred to keep it that way.

Sadly, this one was just a few years older than his eldest daughter and one who had more in common with her, too. If revealed, his connection to her could not only destroy his relationship with his daughter, but his relationship with his church, his community, and worse, his wife.

"Just don't forget," she reminded him, expecting a deposit in her account for her time and performance. If asked, he'd tell you he never paid for sex. He paid for time—time to be alone and to be himself without all the demands of the world. This just turned from business into personal, and he couldn't seem to find his way out of it.

It wasn't that Theodore didn't love ministry or the Lord. He just never factored in how the growing success would start to feel like work and work turning into resentment. Even when he got home, his executive administrative assistant, Donna, wouldn't let up. He could barely sit down in his office at home before she'd quickly run down a list of appearances and events coming up on the phone. And when the church's finances took a hit, that's when he made the biggest mistake of his life—he used his daughter, manipulated her, and now he was filled with regret.

"I'll take care of it," was all he said, hearing his armor

bearer at the door. One glance at his cell and he frowned, wondering why his wife hadn't called. He loved her, loved her dearly. Even if he ignored her most times outside of church or the bedroom. Still, she was loyal just like his daughter Faith, or so he prayed, knowing at all times usually where she was and with whom. Still, something felt off. Valerie was just too quiet.

"Guess I'll call her when I get to the airport," he said to no one in particular, getting up as he went to the bathroom. He stopped though when his chocolate guest snickered. "What, Dashon?" he asked, feeling torn. Hard not to after she spread her legs open, revealing her freshly waxed vagina. It was all perched up and ready for the taking.

"Nothing," she replied with a hiss, as she slipped her slender finger between her glistening lower lips. As soon as she did, the flesh called and he answered based on the swell, the heaviness of his penis that swung, hitting his thigh as he headed toward her. "Dashon, we got to stop this, baby," he said, all the while crawling back into bed. "It was never supposed to go this far, and then you gave him something I have to see all the time. A child, wondering if she's mine."

"Please," she said, dismissively as his hand trailed up her thigh. "You know Kasia Ann's not yours, but trust me, she will forever be provided for because of you. That chump change Denver gives me is worthless. Thanks, baby," she whispered, his lips against hers before his tongue slithered in her mouth like the tongue of a snake.

"Yes, worthless." He laughed, once he pulled back even though most of what he'd acquired was because of him—his sacrifice called prison. Especially since it was him that had sent Dashon Denver's way while he was incarcerated to get information about any dealings he might have possibly had with his daughter once he had forbidden her to have any contact with him. He wasn't so sure that letter worked or if she'd tried sending him letters after being banned from the prison.

Before then, he'd done everything possible to get him arrested and convicted, even had him followed. It was the only way he could get her to focus on Razz. The one that wanted his validation while Denver only wanted Faith. As time grew close for his release, he knew one thing that Denver valued and that was love, especially after depriving him of it.

Dashon and Denver reconnecting, however, wasn't in the plan. Still, once it happened, she shared it with him, and he pressed her to stay on him, keep him distracted and his balls deep and empty into her pussy. He was desperate, and the last thing he needed was for Faith to find out her first love was not only home, but that he was responsible for him being set up and sent to prison.

Then all hell broke loose when Razz's true colors emerged as he began to spiral out of control. While Amber wasn't his first affair, she would probably be his last. That was if the drugs didn't take them out. Something he still wondered how he missed.

Since he was using, he decided to set up an overdose storyline if Razz didn't get it together and before he could reveal all their secrets. He was tired, beyond tired of cleaning up all the little fires that were popping up all over the place, including the one that tried to be released about him. Not only did he spend thirty grand to release photos of Faith and Denver, but he paid forty grand to get rid of the ones of him and Dashon that were sent to his cell weeks earlier.

While Theodore shut the door, Deacon Rueben received a call from Deacon Monroe.

"Where's Theo?" he asked him, his voice sounding stressed.

"He's uh, in the bathroom," he lied. He wasn't sure how long they could keep this lie going since it kept him away from his own wife and children. He was starting to see why Deacon Monroe stepped down, prepared to hand in his own resignation, but he needed the money. And once again, money was the reason many that claimed to love the Lord were failing at showing it.

"The bathroom. Yeah, well tell him to check his phone when he gets out," he grumbled, shaking his head before his eyes met Valerie's when he hung up.

"I don't even care, Shakur. As long as he signs these," she said, pushing him her divorce documents with something else that almost knocked the soul out of his body.

"My God," he whispered. "First the church catching on fire, and now this. Is that his child?"

"No, but the ones before her were. Three abortions and a secret bank account that now has been frozen. May God spare him because Denver may not," she said, patiently waiting for next Sunday's dinner. It was time she got her daughters all in one place and her family on track without the infamous Pastor Theodore Valentine running the show.

"I know you think I should be ecstatic about this since... you know," he said, feeling uneasy whenever he broached the subject about feelings for her. He'd never violate her or her vows, even if he knew he should have done more to get her.

"I do, but I've always known," she said, sighing as their eyes met before he broke the stare. If nothing else, Shakur was loyal. Loyal to a fault as he watched the love of his life fight hard to right her wrongs and repair her relationship with her children. He understood why, but he just couldn't see himself helping her take his best friend down. Not when he knew it would take his best friend away from his wife.

"Oh, forget about feeling guilty," she added, tossing a wave his way. "Always the good guy, right?" she said, smiling at Shakur as he nervously sat next to her.

"It's just… I don't know, Valerie. I've always tried to do the right thing. Always wanted to please God, serve him. Ministry is real to me, helping people, watching them get delivered. I get excited about it," he confessed, as she took his hand.

"I know, Shakur, and God will soon bless you beyond measure for doing just that. Now, no more worrying. I have it from here," she assured him. "Besides, it's about time all these secrets came out. I'm surprised Faith even called me. She's been angry with me for a long time now. For years, to be honest," she said, reminiscing on the day she learned Faith was married. Instead of demanding an annulment, she sat by silently as her husband so called did the work of the Lord.

"Faith will be fine," he told her, albeit with a weak smile. Still, he tried to see God in everything, even in the midst of a man's downfall. That's why God was God and man wasn't. "God is faithful, Valerie. He'll show himself mighty. Don't worry. Please don't."

"That he is. But until he does, let me do what I should have a long time ago. Next Sunday, just make sure you're here for dinner. Faith has bad weather where she is, but God willing, she'll be here too."

"Look, I rather not," he told her, understanding her pain. He wasn't going to talk her out of it since he had bigger fish to fry like how the church was going to recover from this fire. He was over the finance committee, and the funds were a bit off. Mercy worked with him, and every time he said he needed to investigate further, she'd intervene. "You're not worried? Thousands of people depend on Piney Grove. We won't be able to get back in there for months. I just don't see how planning a dinner is going to fix it all."

She took his hand and issued a warm grin. When she did, his eyes crinkled as a soft smile surfaced on his face. Just like that, she'd brought out a smile he'd been fighting. It was then he knew that no matter what, he would always love him some Valerie.

Always.

"It will do just what I need it to do. For once, trust me like you trust God or try to."

Chapter Twenty

"She's in there sleep," Denver whispered as he, Knight, and Queen sat around the dining room table.

Once Faith fell off into a deep slumber, he slipped out and asked Knight to meet him in his man cave. He wasn't too happy either, looking over his shoulder at a knocked out Noel. He was ready to go another round with her when Denver called him up. They weren't too far away, so it took him twenty minutes to get there. By then, the generator was hooked up, and they were huddled up, trying to figure things out. Queen came along too with her kids and husband in tow. Soon, Denver's house was filled with people, and for the first time, it felt like home.

"What did you find out?" he asked Queen as she busily pecked away.

"I'm still researching, sir," she responded, rolling her eyes. "Malachi is not too pleased when he had to come over here, Knight," she grumbled, hearing the rain outside.

"You didn't. I was going to FaceTime you. That was you that wanted to come here. We could have linked up with you after the storm if we needed to, so just chill. Stop trying to have me beat your husband's ass, girl," he told her. "I should beat that shit anyway with all the food you had delivered to my damn place," he fumed. "D, you should have seen it."

"Whatever. The kids wanted to come because they thought Paige and PJ were with Noel," she said, speaking of Noel's niece and nephew. "Once they got to your place and saw they weren't, I knew they'd be inside wanting to eat this or that. So I had to do my thing on Instacart," she replied, defending herself.

"Giving out my address and shit," Knight mumbled. "Bought for an army," he continued. "Then I spent two hours separating it and putting it away only for them to follow me over here."

"I can't help I want to make sure my family eats. Noel is not used to cooking for a tribe," she replied, hitting him where it hurt since she knew he wanted kids.

"Mind your fucking business, Queen," he warned her. "And that was petty as hell."

"I think I see something," she whispered, shifting their attention back to why she was there. She then leaned before tapping quickly on the keys. "And I'm sorry," she said, sighing as she felt awful.

She was still somewhat jealous she had to share Knight with another woman. In fact, she was glad they hadn't had kids yet since Noel was almost seven years his junior. Her brother was ready for kids, even helping her raise hers, but Noel needed more time before she took on such a huge responsibility and one that would have Knight forcing her into being a kept woman. Deep down, she knew that would never fly, but when it was all said and done, she'd never go against her brother, so Noel was in the family to stay.

"Hey, is the warden's name at Petersburg Correctional Warden Calhoun?"

"It is now. He just came on last year. I've been out a few years now. I still send money to a few of the guys in there I was cool with—Beanie Head, Pac, and Jazz," Denver informed her, nodding his head. "I was good keeping to myself, but those three wouldn't leave my ass alone." He laughed. "Even if I was starving and wouldn't take anything from them, they would have someone put food on my bunk if I was in the shower or on the yard, working out."

"Nigga, your name is Rock. You already knew that was going to happen. Why were you surprised?" Knight asked, smirking. "For a while, I couldn't even get shit in there myself. Well, not legally. This fool wouldn't even put my name on the list for six months after I was released."

"For what? You had to get out and see about Queen and King. That would have been hella selfish of me to expect that. Stop playing with me, Knight. I did what I did, and I got what I got."

"Naw, *we* did what we did, and you got punished severely. I'm still trying to figure out why or how Razz's charges got dropped."

"Because of him," Queen said, turning her laptop around and pointing to the name on the computer. "Warden James Ivory."

"Dashon's father? But why? I wasn't even messing with her before I got knocked. The fuck? He had an issue with me then too? I must have bust down one of his old bitches or Dashon used to fuck with Razz," he said, laughing but still confused.

"Then this nigga get caught up with the warden's daughter,'" Knight slid in under his breath, laughing. "Might as well still be in prison since all they do is fight," Knight teased, trying to lighten the mood. "I love Kay though with her bad ass," he said, when Denver slammed his fists on the table, feeling played.

"Alright, motherfucker. Didn't you tell me that you had this flown in from Australia? Noel loved this damn table the second she saw it. Hell, I just bought two of them hitting the store up online," he said, looking at Denver like he'd lost his mind.

"Fuck this damn table, Knight," he growled.

"Hey, relax. Just calm down, you two," Queen said, lowering both of her hands as she took deep breaths slowly, in and out, coaching them to do the same. "Yes, just take a deep breath. The enemy is not in this room. Remember that."

"Fuck," Denver released. "Look, I apologize, bro," Denver said, reaching over and giving Knight dap. "Head's spinning, yo. I was out of line for that."

"Naw, you're good. I understand. A motherfucker get me knocked and take Noel away from me, the entire world won't rest as long as I'm breathing. I'll stay fucking shit up on God," he replied, looking Queen's way with a scowl on his face.

"I don't know what that little girl got between her legs, but I don't want it," Queen mumbled as Knight sat back and smirked.

"Listen, D. Stay focused. You took a hit and you've bounced back. You were bouncing back before you knew what you know now."

"I know," he said, stressed, as he rubbed the waves on top of his head. "I just feel confused."

"That hoodoo pussy Dashon gave you. That's what has you confused," Knight teased, smiling. "Shoot." He laughed.

"I thought the nigga moved in with the warden he was there so much," he said, smiling as he looked at Queen. "I even brought him some food out there a few times. Soap, change of underwear too."

"Knight, are you serious? You could have gotten in trouble or worse—locked up too," Queen fussed. "Why would you be that stupid?"

"Shit, the answer is easy," he said, looking across at Denver. "For him." He knew with Denver he'd never have to even ask if the shoe was on the other foot. "And I'd take that time any day for him, too," he said with conviction as Denver dropped his head, all in his feelings.

"Yeah, well I'm confused about why the warden is so invested in some kid no one knew he even knew ," Denver said, as he leaned his head back as he looked up at the ceiling.

"Was he ever a member of Piney Grove?" Queen asked when Denver's head shot her way.

"Damn it. That's it," he whispered, remembering one day Pastor Valentine came to the prison. He found out he was there counseling a few inmates when he saw him down at the end of the hall talking to Warden Ivory.

"He did?" Knight asked, wondering since he never remembered seeing him there.

"I was leaving the clinic. Fucked my hand up punching a wall. I called out to him, but his back was to me. When I yelled out at him again, I saw the two of them shake hands, and then he started walking further away. Psych nurse said he was a visiting chaplain that came through sometimes for psych inmates. I figured he didn't hear me since a bunch of inmates were calling his name too."

"You think Dashon knows their connection?" Knight

probed, looking Queen's way. He knew she knew more, just unsure how much to say in front of his boy. They'd always had that sister/brother bond that transcended beyond spoken words. When Knight slightly shook his head, she closed the laptop.

"I don't know, and now there's a child involved," she said, reaching for Denver's hand and taking it. "I say let me do a little more research, but for now, let's get some rest," she suggested before she yawned. "And I need to save my battery."

"Yeah, what Queen said," Knight agreed. "And we have two generators. I can charge it, sis. Trust me. We're good around here with two. His ass kind of cheap, so you know I had to bring mine," he replied, when Denver told him to kiss his ass. "Naw, I'm about to kiss *her* ass," he said, pointing at Noel who was snoring and drooling.

"Ugh, I still can't believe this is my brother," she groaned. "I'm going to bed."

"Thanks, baby girl. Good looking out," he told her, smiling as he kissed her on the cheek.

"No problem. You know I'll do anything for family, and Denver, baby, you're family."

"Appreciate that," he said when Knight poured him a drink. "I need this for real," he said, sighing.

"And then put that shit on ice, D," Knight told him. "We're different men now with more to lose. I promise you, we'll get down to the bottom of it. But for now, keep everything right here."

"Not for long because Kay's granddaddy about to be left stinking somewhere. I'll take that time. I'll fucking take it," he declared, getting up and pouring himself a drink. "So damn putting it on ice for long."

"Then that settles it. I guess I'll take that time, too," he said, dapping him up once more before they all decided to head to bed. "But maybe we won't have to. Let Queen get on it tomorrow. I'm sure we'll get to the bottom of it."

Chapter Twenty-One

"I told you I didn't need a chauffeur, Rellon," Joy told him, tossing a few items in her bag. "And if I did, who said I wanted it to be you?"

"Joy Joy, not now. One, I'm here for you. Chased your ass down, and a good thing I came before you took off. Have you seen that fucking weather? Two, Faith's my sister."

"You wouldn't have to chase anything down. You left, but hey, you did what was best, right?" she said sarcastically, looking around for her keys. Rell wasn't sure where she called herself really going after examining her place. She had clothes everywhere and a few sex toys that made him fume. "So you can excuse yourself and let me return back to my real life. I'm not fucking with you like that, remember?" she spat, switching her tiny hips as she went through her condo grabbing a few more things.

"That mouth is still hot, I see," he told her, plopping down on her sofa. She sucked her teeth every time he looked her way. In fact, the more she did, the more he had time to indulge in her beauty.

Even in a rush, she effortlessly threw together one of her outfits that accentuated her flawless rich chocolate complexion, wearing a coral top that crisscrossed in the front and back along with a tan, pink and peach patched skirt that flowed effortless down her long frame. Her hair was cut low and texturized like Jada Pinkett, showing off her cheekbones that complemented her heart-shaped mouth and thin, yet sexy lips.

"Pretty ass," he said, before he dodged a shoe she threw his way. "Aye, girl. You already know a fight with me is one you will never win, Joy Joy. Keep playing," he warned her. "In fact, you got two minutes to finish this show you're putting on. Trying to entice me," he told her, standing up as she approached him smiling.

"You mean like this," she said, rising on her tippy toes as she tugged on his shirt to pull his mouth down to hers. Just when he went to peck her on the lips, she turned her head, causing his to land on her cheek. "You must think I'm crazy," she snapped, pushing him away. "With a friend like Razz, pussy probably stays in your mouth."

"The fuck you even talking about?"

"Exactly what I said. Now, you can go wherever you came from. Thanks for popping up unannounced, but you can leave now," she told him, giving him her back as she located her keys when she kicked a shoe box. In an instant, she was in his arms, her arms flailing as she screamed and kicked. With ease, Rell not only carried her and her luggage out with one hand, but he also locked the door with the other.

"I'm going to fuck you up!" she screamed all the way until they made it to his truck. By the time he'd put her down and pushed her against the passenger's door, Joy was out of breath.

He then took her mouth, forcing her to calm down. What started out as a rough and choppy kiss morphed into a slow, sensual one that literally took her breath away. When he applied a few pecks before pulling away, Joy was breathless and speechless, a rare sight that caused Rell to laugh.

"I've been wanting to do that shit since I saw you. Now calm the hell down, and get in this fucking truck, Joy Joy. Faith's my sister too, and while I made some fucked up decisions, I always made them with you in mind. I left for you, so you could have time to live your life and not get tied down with a motherfucker like me. What the fuck did I have back then besides being big as fuck and someone who could fight? Huh, Joy Joy?" he challenged her, cupping her face.

"I didn't want anything," she managed to get out, her chest heaving up and down.

"Well, you for damn sure should have. Now you have it, and now that I'm back, no more fucking IG videos. Don't think I don't see niggas in them comments trying to buy more than clothes," he told her, slipping his hand around her body to open the door. "Yeah, I'm proud of you Joy Joy. Keep doing your thing. Pastor did good when it came to you. Even if he can't see it right now. Never not be you because a motherfucker can't accept you. Even me."

"Wow." She laughed, easing inside once he opened the door for her. "You watch me on IG?"

"Shit, try me buying about a hundred outfits too under some lame IG page, girl," he admitted, causing them both to laugh. "We doing a pop up shop or something to sell all that. What I look like having a bunch of female clothes?" he said, buckling her in.

"Maybe a man in love. A dumb ass one who just couldn't admit he went about things the wrong way," she said, beaming.

She had no idea he'd been supporting her all along when he showed her the IG account.

"Now sit back, and let's get to Mason. That's messed up how they're doing Faith, man, and Rock's good people. It had to have been a reason they linked up or hell, who knows."

"Wait, you're not mad?" she asked him, eyeing him suspiciously.

"To be honest, Faith is too good for Razz. I just wish they'd both would have kept it a G with each other over the years. Now he's doing whatever he's doing—"

"Please," she stopped him, holding up her hand in his face. "You know what he's doing. Stop pretending like you're snitching," she shot back as he walked away, laughing. He wasn't trying to fight with her about Razz. He was too busy trying to make things right with his own girl.

"I ain't playing with you, Joy Joy," he said, getting inside on the driver's side. "My point is people waste time when time itself is never controlled by us. So why not spend it doing what you want and with who you want to spend it with?"

"Hmph. Ask yourself that," she sassed before he tugged her chin and leaned over.

"Don't have to. I'm fixing it right now, Joy Joy."

Chapter Twenty-Two

After hours of being up, Queen kept digging to get more information. She just couldn't go to sleep after what she'd learned earlier. Unlike King, who took the lead all of their lives, getting money to provide for them, Queen was the strategist, the planner, the thinker. The one that wanted more than a "right now'" solution. She wanted long term wins. She wanted success.

While Knight back in the day hit the streets hustling, she kept her nose stuck in a book. Foster care may have been a crutch to some, but it was a ladder for her, and a law school degree years later. Now she was chief legal counsel for their company, so if anyone could sniff out a snake and eliminate him, it was Queen.

"Still up?" Denver inquired, sneaking up on her after hearing her peck on her laptop.

"Yeah, sorry. I woke you up, huh? And announce yourself next time." She laughed.

"Un huh." He laughed. He'd always been light on his feet.

Had to be to survive. "And naw, not really. I'm still… I don't know, confused," he admitted, wondering why anyone would be that invested in hurting him. He honestly just felt violated.

"Yeah, well I can't explain the why, but I can explain the who. But here's where it gets interesting," she shared, waving him over. She just prayed Knight wouldn't be mad, but she had to tell Denver after she saw the pain on his face, heard it in his voice, too. "This Warden Ivory has ties to Razz because he's his father."

"Queen, get the fuck out of here," Denver replied, in shock. "His father?"

"But"—she said, holding up her finger—"no one knows. Well, not publicly since his name is not on the birth certificate. Hospital records show the night his mother was brought in under the influence, a male by the name of Justice Ivory signed her in. He was even listed as her emergency contact number and paid cash to cover anything she needed. On the day of her discharge, Razz is signed out to him since his mother needs to go to detox, and the release documents identify him as the father."

"Un-fucking-believable. So that's how he gets off," Denver said to himself, dragging his hand down his mouth. "And probably why I saw Pastor Valentine with the warden all those years ago."

"Maybe, maybe not, but the entire family has secrets." *Like maybe your daughter isn't even your daughter,"* she thought to herself, holding back some information she wasn't sure she needed to share.

"This sounds like some *Lifetime Movie Network* movie drama. Just shut it down," he told her, his mind blown from what he'd just heard. "I'm good," he said, nodding his head as the rain continued to pound roughly against the windows.

"Get some rest, Queen. And thanks. A nigga needed to know that, but I got it from here," he said, pouring himself another drink.

"Hey, for what it was worth, it's better knowing than not knowing, right? At least you know he took a loss too."

"Who, Razz?"

"I mean, yeah. His father didn't raise him. His mother's an addict and now he's lost the woman that seems to have always belonged to you. Truthfully, you all have more in common than you don't," she said, referring to Denver also being raised by his grandmother.

"I hear you, Queen," was all he said, as he sat in the dark after she decided to get an hour or two of sleep before the kids woke up.

Hours later, they all sat around. The kids were playing board games with Noel and their father, while Queen was in the kitchen making sandwiches and cutting fresh fruit. Even exhausted, she made sure her family came first while Faith sat in a daze, resting against Denver's chest.

"Tell me what you're thinking?" he whispered in her ear. "No judgement."

"How my life will never be the same again," she replied, thinking about the request that she'd received from her mother. "As soon as the roads are clear, I have to go."

"Word?" he replied, assuming she meant to her husband. "Well, you two are still married," he added, nodding his head, a tad bit disappointed, but he was a realist. He had bigger issues to handle himself, starting with his daughter's trifling grandfather and possibly Faith's father.

"Oh, not to him," she quickly corrected him, sitting up. "My mother has requested my presence next Sunday for dinner," she said, watching a smile appear on his face. "Yes, one probably with her Mexican cornbread and infamous lemonade."

"Miss Val and that damn lemonade." He smiled, dragging his hand down his mouth. "You know I have that on my juice menu, but you was playing. I couldn't even let you test it out."

"Well, how about we both go to handle that when we can… that is, if you don't mind being seen with me," she added, taking a peek at the blogs herself when she woke up.

The captions were a bit cruel, suggesting how the Streeters were frauds, fake Christians, making millions using God's name. It stung a little, but not enough for her to care to comment. She was more interested in what the ladies said when they saw Denver, and she had to admit that they looked really cute as they stared into each other's eyes.

"I know your daughter's mother is not too pleased," she added, trying to gauge if it mattered once she saw the pictures for herself. "I haven't seen you on your phone though."

"Girl, I checked on Grams and my daughter. Outside of that, her mother is none of my concern. As for what she saw, trust me. She has more to be concerned about than who I'm with," he told her, stopping short of revealing what else he knew. He advised Queen not to share, so for now, only him, her, and Knight knew about it.

"Okay," Faith sang, rising up and looking down at him. "I'm hungry. Want to go raid the kitchen and head back to the room, because Queen's tripping?" She laughed.

"I heard that!" she yelled, causing everyone to chime in as Denver stood up too. "Find any reason to ditch us, Miss Thing," Queen said, appearing at the kitchen door. "I've been washing and cutting up fruit while you two beauties have been lollygagging around and resting. Go on now," she told her, shooing her and Denver off. "I'll have the kids bring you something to eat," she said, giving them that look like she knew they were going in there to do more. Besides that one heated moment when they first got there, though, they'd been on their best behavior.

"Un uh, not even," Faith said, laughing as Denver slapped her ass.

"Not yet," he added, taking her hand as he led her to the bedroom.

"I'm the godmother!" Noel yelled out when they slammed the door. "Mean asses," she playfully huffed before she called out, "Uno!"

Chapter Twenty-Three

"Sweetheart," Pastor Valentine said, rushing in the house to greet his wife. "I came as soon as I could," he continued before kissing her cheek as he caught his breath. "I tell you, if it's not one thing, it's another," he added, taking off his coat at the door along with his shoes.

"You got that right," she said, smiling as he stopped and took a deep breath. "But it's a good thing we have insurance. As soon as I got the call, I had Donna pull up all the policies. All we need is the report from the fire department, and then we can move on to getting estimates and then repairs," she said, when Deacon Munroe appeared.

"Shakur," he said, shocked as he looked from his wife then back to his best friend. "I didn't know you were here."

"Oh, I decided not to bother you. You were doing the Lord's work, so I called him," she said. "Let's go into the dining room and go over a few things," she said calmly as he lifted both brows.

"Uh, sure. Sha?" he said, motioning him over before she lifted her hand.

"Shakur is wrapping up a few things. While he does, go change, and dress comfortably. I'll even go with you to make sure you don't take too long. Oh, how I've missed you, honey," she cooed, as she slipped her arm through his.

"Okay, honey. Anything you say," he said, repeating her term of endearment as they headed toward their bedroom. "Have you heard from Mercy? Anything financial, she should be a part of."

"Later. We'll call her in later," was all she said as Shakur took a deep breath before he went to pray.

"Razz, you better pick the fuck up and now," his father-in-law threatened him, hiding in the bathroom. He'd already showered and shaved and now he lied, saying his stomach was troubling him as he sat on the toilet. A fire meant repairs, but more money would be needed to carry them until then. This was a perfect time to get him and his daughter together to put on a show in the park. He had it all mapped out in his head, needing him to answer. "The hell is going on," he fussed lowly, calling Dashon next.

He was going to need more of her and soon after the greeting he'd received. They'd both flown back in town on different flights to Jonestown, but hers should have landed by now.

"Baby," he said, quickly. "Have you heard about the church? A fire, baby."

"I have," she said, pulling up into her father's driveway.

He'd been calling her all week, and instead of calling him back, she decided to go see him in person. They weren't necessarily on the best terms, but he was still her father. "I'm so sorry, Theo baby. How bad is it?"" she asked, watching a smiling Kasia Ann in the rearview mirror. When she giggled, Dashon did too.

"Oh, you have the baby. Happy I see?" he added, remembering when he first became a father.

"Very. She had a good time with her aunt. Denver's not good for shit when it comes to communicating, but his sister definitely helps out. We don't get along, but as soon as I call and mention Kay, she's right there."

"Yeah, that sounds like Brianna. She and Faith were close at one point," he mentioned before his wife called out to him. "Listen, let's meet up later. I don't know what the hell is going on over here, but I'm going to need some pussy," he whispered, stroking his length as he smiled. He just couldn't get enough of Dashon, and sadly, the only guilt he felt was leaving her.

"Soon that won't be enough, Theodore," she said, looking at her ten thousand dollar Cartier watch with canary yellow diamonds.

"I know, Dashon. I know, but it's complicated. Don't—" he said and stopped when he heard the doorknob turning. "Gotta go."

"I was wondering if you were okay," his wife said, noticing he was sweating. "Need something for your stomach?"

"No, not at all. Rough flight, baby. Bumpy ride had it messed up, but I'm okay now. I'll be out in a few. Tell Shakur don't start without me," he said as she slowly eased back out and closed the door.

"Oh, he won't," she said quietly to herself. "Besides, I want you to see everything we need to go over and how you've finally lost everything you've ever worked for," she continued, smiling as she walked away.

Chapter Twenty-Four

"*Breaking news, gospel singer, Razz Streeter, was found unconscious in his hotel room. Authorities are not saying what happened or who alerted them, but he's been flown to Jonestown University. We also have learned that Amber Rhinestone was air lifted there too," Ryda announced, as she smirked at Seagal.*

"Yeah, to those out there that know how to send up a prayer, add Razz and Amber to your prayer list. As more information comes in, we'll bring it to you, but it's a time for prayer. My heart goes out to his wife, Faith Streeter. Faith, girl, keep your head up," Seagal said as Ryda rolled her eyes.

"Damn, Razz," Rell said, as Joy rested her head on his shoulder. They weren't even on the highway yet when they heard about Razz and Amber. She'd somehow reconnected with Razz as soon as Rell took off to spend some time with Joy. He wasn't buying her ignoring Razz and now he knew why. They both were powder and pill heads, just like Denver had predicted all those years ago.

Skull, another one of their security, had hit him up before it was leaked to the public, devastated when he discovered them unresponsive. After canvassing the room, he'd swiped it clean of the pills or any signs of cocaine residue on the bathroom sink, dresser and living room table. They all dibbled and dabbled in drugs to stay alert. All except for Rell who sat blaming himself.

"I messed up, Joy Joy. I should have made him leave with me."

"To do what? Go win my sister back or fight Denver?" she spat, sitting up with an attitude. "Look, I'm sorry he and his little boo thing are not doing well, but what do you expect, Rellon? To keep putting Razz first?"

"Baby, I'm not even saying that. I'm saying for once I just slid on him when I knew no one around would hold this nigga accountable. Some people need that, Joy Joy," he said, dropping his head back with closed eyes. "For years, it was me and Faith. Now, it's just me."

"And what about me?" she asked, feeling slighted.

"I fucked up when it came to you, but at sixteen, Joy Joy, I was right not even touching you. And when you turned legal, all I wanted to do was touch you, love on you and shit. But was I ready?" he said, taking her hand as he kissed the back of it. "Fuck no, and neither were you. I won't say I couldn't have handled that better, but when we finally did have sex, damn girl, I was a goner," he said, smiling as she playfully nudged him. "Why do you think we're two messed up, toxic ass people? Young, sex game lit, and out here just living wild. How could we have made it when we stayed on some Ike and Tina Turner shit?"

"Boy, you have never hit me," she shot back with squinted eyes.

"Exactly, it was your ass." He laughed. "Always fighting me."

"So?" she said, shrugging her shoulders. "What about now?" she probed. When she did, they both saw a man in a lab coat she assumed was Razz's attending physician approached them.

"I'm here with you, baby. It's going to be okay," Joy assured him as they both stood up to greet him.

"Family of Raziel Streeter?"

"Yes, I'm his father," they heard a man say, walking up and taking his hand. "His father and sister," he said, pointing to a beautiful, dark skinned woman that looked familiar to the both of them. She was crying, and all Joy could wonder was if that sister title was a secret code for another bitch Razz was dealing with, pursing her lips. "And this here is his best friend. Feel free to speak freely in front of him."

"And my girl," Rell chimed in, staring at the man suspiciously. He recognized him from back in the day but wasn't sure what was going on. He gave Rell a look that told him they'd discuss it later while the little girl in the woman's arms squealed and laughed. "She's cute."

"Thanks. I guess Razz's niece. I'm Dashon," she said, glaring at her father. "Apparently we have a lot to talk about. Nice to meet you," she said, extending her hand. While Rell accepted it, Joy gave her a fake smile, tilting her head.

"No thanks," she said. She was not interested in meeting anyone affiliated with Razz, to which Dashon laughed and shook her head.

"Well, now we know who's all who, let's talk," the doctor said as Razz's father fought back tears. He'd been battling for years on how to tell his son what happened and why he could never be there. As soon as he heard of him overdosing, he knew his time was running out, and he couldn't wait any longer.

Chapter Twenty-Five

"How are you feeling?" Denver asked Faith as they entered the highway. Since their reconnection two weeks prior, so much had happened. What started out as her getaway to figure out next steps turned into a second chance to love and finally letting the past go. She never factored in that letting go meant Razz overdosing.

Now the blogs treated his affair and her sighting with Denver like last year's news. The latest was whether or not Razz would make it out of the hospital alive while other women he'd been with over the years came forward.

While Faith knew he'd been with others, watching it unfold in front of the world was eye opening and painful. She was prepared to kill Razz herself if he lived, until Denver reminded her the one thing everyone seemed to have forgotten—no man is without sin and all men struggled with demons.

His was just women, drugs, and it seemed, feeling unloved. His inflated ego was proof of it, which was now a part of his downfall. It seemed like that talk with Queen did sink in just a little. They had even all prayed together before they left. They'd accepted that she was the only person that could speak on his care in terms of resuscitating him or not was Faith, but she wasn't going without him. A task she really wasn't up for or wanted, but it was her duty as his wife once she'd received the call.

"Scared, confused," she admitted, looking at the sun as it rose. "How did I miss that?" she asked Denver, wondering if she ever knew Razz at all. "Drugs? What kind of wife doesn't know that her husband's using drugs? Gosh, I feel like I failed him," she admitted, her emotions all over the place. "I guess I didn't care enough to care enough, if that makes sense, you know?"

"Naw, Mouse. I can't let you think like that when it comes to how you moved," he replied, refusing to let her carry that burden on her own. "You realized the things you were doing weren't things you ever cared about in the first place," he said. "And that's the truth. It mattered to your father," he said, choosing to leave it at that. "You going now is because you love and fear God. And once you made those vows, you signed up for it."

"I did I suppose," she said and sighed, thinking of her father. Her parents made those vows too, but the more she thought about their marriage, it felt more like an arrangement and contract. It was also what pushed the wedge between her and her family except Joy who alerted her what had happened before the news began to spread.

"And in the future? How do you feel about getting married again?" he asked her, surprising her.

"Well. Uh, I don't know," she said, feeling his hold on her

hand tightened as he smiled. She couldn't help but smile too, processing what he'd just asked her. It wasn't a proposal, but it was him expressing what he wanted for them some day.

"I guess whoever the man is would have to properly get to know me, date me first, and if it's in God's will, I'd eagerly say yes. And he would have to accept the life I've established, my ministry. It takes a secure man to live in my world if the blogs had to tell it." She laughed. "Now, what about you? I think I read something about you being engaged at one point. I won't lie, I did some social media snooping myself," she admitted, patting the top of his hand. "Your name is trending, sir. You never mentioned an engagement with Dashon."

"Hell, I can't mention what was never true," he told her as he sucked his teeth. "*She* wanted that, but I kind of always knew that spot belonged to someone else," he said, looking her way and grinning as Faith dropped her head before staring out the window.

"Does she know? The person the spot belonged to?"

"Fuck yeah, Mouse. I just told her," he said, when she snatched her hand away and playfully punched him.

"Denver, you scared me." She laughed. "Don't do that again," she whined, as he pulled her over to him, kissing her forehead.

"The only thing that's scary, Mouse, is you and Kay not getting along. But my lil' mama is cool. You'll love her, and she'll love you," he said, kissing her forehead once more.

"I pray so," she whispered. "Her mother is your first child's mother, but I'm here to tell you that Faith Caroline will be the last."

"Look at you bossing up on me. Savage ass," he said, feeling full of hope. He hadn't felt like that since the day she entrusted him to not only attend to her wound from the wasp bite, but to hold on to her heart.

Truly, they were locked in love… forever.

Epilogue

A Year Later

"I now pronounce you husband and wife. You may kiss your bride, sir," the pastor said to Deacon Munroe as he lifted her veil. Valerie had never looked more beautiful in all the years he'd known her.

"Alright now, Mama! Get it!" Joy called out before Faith shushed and nudged her. "What? Girl, mama about to turn up," she said while Mercy snickered. "See, even Mercy knows."

"Still encouraging her, right?" Faith asked her as their mother, and Deacon Munroe waved to everyone in the church as they marched outside to take photos.

"Joy's been loud. Trust me, she doesn't need my encouragement," Mercy replied as all three stood at the front of the church misty-eyed. It had been a long journey, but all of the secrets were out.

"Whatever, I'm kind of tired of the both of you. Let me go find my boyfriend with his fine behind," she said, walking off and swishing her hips just so Rell could take her to a bathroom and help her release all of her pent-up tension. He still hadn't had sex with her since they were trying celibacy. But that didn't mean that they didn't do other things.

"Guess that leaves two of us," Faith said, looking over at an emotional yet smiling Mercy. "I'm glad we're close again. I missed you, Mercy Annabelle."

"Oh, God. There you go with the middle names," she said, pushing her when Faith kissed her playfully on the cheek. "Now let's see if we can get through this reception dinner. God knows we don't need what happened the last time we were at Mama's house."

"Say that," Faith agreed before they took each other by the hand and headed outside. Joy was going to miss the photoshoot, but what else was new when it came to Joy, the rebel Valentine sister?

"Now that we all are here, Theodore, why don't you say grace," his wife suggested, looking around at their formal dining room table that easily sat ten people.

All of their children were there—Faith, Joy, and Mercy along with Denver, Rellon, and Mercy's husband, Paul. Then there was Donna, the church's executive administrative assistant, and Deacon Munroe.

All had been required to attend, and despite the unknown reasons why, First Lady Valerie's lemonade was always a draw. That day, she gave her husband a chance to tell the truth and the whole truth, but he never would give up his hand. Painfully, Valerie had to move on to plan B where all of their skeletons came crashing out the closet. Once he concluded grace and all replied amen, Valerie stood up and smiled.

"The past few weeks have been hell, pure hell, I tell you, but guess what has been more than that? My marriage to your father," she said, looking at her daughters.

"Ba-baby, wait a minute," he managed to get out as he stood up, knocking his chair over. "What are you talking about?"

"Oh, well I'm so glad you asked," she said, reaching down and picking up an envelope. She handed it to him, but not before she said, "Oh, copies have been made. Those are yours. Read them quietly I suggest," she told him with great joy.

"Copies? And for what?" As he slowly pulled them out, she looked to Donna and asked that she stand. Then she looked to Mercy and asked her to do the same.

"Mercy, baby? Please know that I love you, honey. I love you so much."

"I uh, love you too, Mama." She laughed nervously, feeling uncomfortable as Donna's eyes reached hers and then her mother's.

"And Donna," she said, reaching over and taking her hand. "I'm sorry. I'm so sorry… I was wrong, very wrong," she released, her voice cracking as she began to cry. "But I thought I was doing the right thing."

"Valerie, please don't," Theodore demanded of his wife while looking at Donna.

"I didn't, Theodore. You did, and you've been making this child pay for it ever since," she told him, looking Mercy's way. "I didn't know how you knew, but I can tell you when it was clear to me you did. You developed a hard heart against your sisters, you saw fault in them, always wanting to be the chosen child. I couldn't understand how you three were so close, and then one day I woke up and you weren't."

"Mama?" Joy interrupted, her voice shaky as Rell took her hand. He knew if anyone was about to set it off, it would be his Joy Joy. "What's going on?" she asked when Donna apologized to Mercy. "What did you do, Miss Donna?" she probed while Rell whispered to Denver he needed a drink.

"I-I'm her mother," she revealed, causing everyone to speak out, talking across each other confused.

"Miss Donna, no," Faith said, covering her mouth. She often was said to be another Valentine like she was their mother's sister, but it was all starting to make sense. The trips where Mercy hung out with Donna, paid for her dancing lessons as she called her her godmother, volunteered at the school in the classes Mercy attended. She was around, always around. They all figured it was because she was Mercy's godmother, but now they knew it was more.

Pastor Theodore had to pay her parents off and plenty, her father a retired general in the military. He trusted him with his daughter who was now madly in love. Valerie had just had Faith, and since sex wasn't something on her priority list, soon, Donna became his outlet, and Mercy was conceived. That and postpartum depression that somewhat forced Valerie to stay.

"I have something to say too," Mercy released, tears cascading down her cheeks when she looked at Faith. "I-I'm so, so sorry, Faith," she whispered. "I never meant to hurt you. I swear I didn't. You nor Denver. You know I love you like a brother," she pleaded when her husband Paul stood up, confused.

"Baby, what is going on? What did you do to Faith and Denver?" he asked, while Faith looked at Denver with the "I told you so" look as he dropped his head. He believed her. He always did. He just couldn't understand why while Mercy begged her husband just to have a seat.

"I did something I need to share. Just listen, please," she asked of him as he looked around while her father sat in a daze. "I'm responsible for the letter that was sent to Denver, breaking things off. It was me. I even faked the journal, Faith. It was to push you into Razz's arms if you felt I liked Denver. You were always like that, so giving, so selfless, and then…" she said, sniffling when she looked at her father. "I set that fire, Mama," she continued as her father's face fell flat, his eyes blinking periodically as he felt his world falling apart. It was to

help the church recoup money. With all the scandal and Faith and Razz no longer helping out, things were tight. "The church needed the money. I was trying to help back then and now, Mama. Daddy needed me," she confessed, her chest heaving up and down as she began to wail.

"Sweetheart, you were a child," her mother Valerie said, coming over to her and taking her into her arms. "And for what it's worth, it's not your fault. None of this is," she assured her, holding her tightly as she cried uncontrollably. "And for the record, I've never loved you any less. Heck, I even blamed myself," she said, staring at Theodore with glassy eyes, filled with pain. "I kept telling myself I wasn't nurturing my husband enough, loving him enough. Didn't even know I had postpartum depression. I couldn't even speak freely about why I was so down after Faith, and then I learned—"

"Enough!" their father barked, out of nowhere, tossing the envelope down on the table. "It was your ass, huh? You son of a bitch!" he spat, looking at his best friend, Shakur. "You always wanted Valerie; couldn't help I not only got the bitch you wanted but got her to marry me and to have my kids. Yeah, this is all you. Got pissed she stayed with me after Mercy, huh?" He laughed, shaking his head. He was so worked up, his mind racing as his lies were tumbling out of the closet one after the other. He was totally oblivious to Denver who'd stood up and walked over to him before he tapped him on the shoulder.

When he looked his way, Denver gave him a quick right to the jaw followed by a quicker and harder left with his fist to his stomach. Everyone screamed, while glasses and plates were being knocked over, as everyone dropped to the floor. Everyone that is except Rell who whispered, shaking his head as he picked up his lemonade. "This right here is good, Miss Valerie. What the hell you put in this?" he asked, laughing as Denver kept whooping Pastor Valentine's ass.

"Want to tell them about why Razz got off and I went to prison, motherfucker?" Denver barked, hovering over him before kicking him the

stomach. "Want to tell them why Faith thought I didn't want her?" he seethed, spittle flying all over him as he lay on the floor.

"Mercy may have wrote that letter you had her send to me, but your bitch ass had Faith removed from the list. I was trying to understand why Warden Ivory would do that after his son got off, but then it hit me."

"Wait, who's the warden's son?" Faith asked, looking around at Rell, then her mother and Deacon Munroe. No one said a thing because no one knew anything at the table except Rell and Joy. Rell was trying to stay in Joy's good graces, keeping quiet. As for Joy, she'd finally spoken to Dashon, but dared that bitch to even whisper a word in the air in Faith's direction. It had been weeks, and not even Denver had heard from her.

"Razz, baby. The warden, Kay's grandfather, is Razz's father," he told her when he kicked her father in the mouth who had started to laugh. "That shit's funny, motherfucker? Yeah, I found out he owed you. You helped get him on at that prison. Worked with the local police to clean up his file. See, he had it rough like me and his own son, but he wanted to make a difference. He was your little project at Piney Grove, and once you found out that was his son, you cashed in on that favor, motherfucker."

"Baby, go see if there's some Hennessy around here," Rell suggested to Joy when their mother begged Denver not to hit him again.

"Miss Valerie, he took my life from me. Faith, my Mouse. You see her?" he screamed, tears running down his face. "That's my heart right there. He took her from me!" he repeated, choked up as her father laughed even more.

"Oh, please," he released, coughing as blood spurted from his mouth. "She's nothing to you, just like Dashon. That pussy you had is mine now. Matter of fact, you might want to get a DNA test," he added, when Denver snatched his nine millimeter from his waist and aimed it at him.

"Denver, nooooo!" Faith screamed before he pulled the trigger.

"I thought you weren't carrying. I still can't believe you shot at my father," Faith whispered as Denver grabbed her hand at the door. She was referring to him and Knight adjusting their burners underneath their tuxedos before they took pictures.

"I just nicked his ass on the ear. Motherfucker is deaf as hell though," he said, laughing.

"You're so mean," she whispered. "And trust me, Razz is not even thinking about me. You don't need a gun here," she said, noticing him at a table with Amber and his family.

He'd done almost a year of inpatient and then outpatient treatment once he pulled through. He was attending NA meetings and even had a sponsor. Amber had recovered sooner and was now a peer counselor at the substance abuse halfway house. There she continued to do makeup and hair as clients transitioned out into the world while giving her testimony.

She and Razz were now married and expecting their first child. As for Razz and Faith, they no longer recorded or performed together, but they continued to generate revenue from their prior music career together and decided to be cordial. Cordial meant an invite to her mother's wedding just to prove they could all be in a room at the same time to co-exist.

He'd been staying close to home, doing more local shows. He'd even started a boys' club, working with disadvantaged youth at the community center while Faith had moved back to Mason with Denver. They didn't live together just yet, but marriage was in their future. For now, they both were working tirelessly at learning how to love each other without remembering all of the pain.

Faith had her own record label, and she and Denver just signed a contract with *Bravo* for their own reality show, *The Daniels Have that Juice*. Though not married, the journey would follow them getting there while showing Faith and Denver at his juice shop, *A Juice to Love*.

"May I have this dance, Faith Daniels?" he asked after they'd taken pictures and entered the reception hall. Couples were already dancing on the floor as everyone waited for the bride and the groom.

"Yes, you may," she replied when Noel came over and bumped up against her arm. She was such a tomboy, rough yet ladylike when it counted as she smiled wearing a soft lavender gown.

"You're next, heifer," she said, giving Denver that look.

"What? It's not me that's holding it up. Talk to your girl," he said, sucking his teeth. "See, Mouse. Stop making me look like the bad guy. Yo, Knight, come get your girl," he called out to his friend that shook his head no. "This nigga. Scary ass."

"No, we agreed to wait until Kasia Ann could walk down the aisle straight without being distracted or having a temper tantrum," she reminded him, causing him to smirk.

"Baby, Kay's a bad ass. Always will be a bad ass. She will *never* walk down any aisle without being distracted or having a temper tantrum. It's not my fault though. She got that rebellious spirit from her mother," he said, ignoring Dashon who also sat at the table where Razz and their father were. Denver allowed to let the warden live, but he did make sure he resigned from any correctional position of power or in the community.

As for him and Dashon, they weren't exactly on speaking terms, but they spoke just enough to coparent their daughter. As for Pastor Valentine, he was doing forty five years for money laundering, tax evasion, and sleeping with a minor. Although just shy of eighteen, he'd long ago pursued Dashon who wanted nothing more than to be the next Mrs. Theodore Valentine. He wasn't sure what contact they had, if any, but

Denver didn't give a fuck. As long as his child wasn't around him.

"Grams, you're good?" he asked his grandmother who was sitting at the table with his sister. "B, what's up, ma?"

"Just finished popping your daughter's leg. Want her?" she asked, patting her back as she fell asleep across her lap.

"I'll get her as soon as she gets up, but for now, I got to stunt in front of that nigga and let him know Mouse is back home with daddy," he said, winking his eye.

"Baby," Faith groaned, covering her face as she blushed. "He won't even speak to me."

"And he motherfucking shouldn't," he told her seriously. "It's bad for his health. Damn that," he corrected himself. "His life."

"Faith, hold him so I can whoop his behind," his grandmother said. He then took Faith's hand and quickly pulled her to the dancefloor.

"I love you, Faith Caroline. I swear I do," he confessed, eyeing her breasts that sat up nicely in her soft canary yellow gown once they were alone. Her hair was longer and all black again, her tresses resting on each side of her face with a part down the middle.

"I love you more, Denver Daniels. You know we're locked in this thing forever, right? What do they call us?" she asked him, as he sucked his teeth. "Na uhhh," she sang. "What's the name?"

"Fenver," he grumbled, and she laughed. "The kind of shit is that, Mouse?"

"Well, it's better than Daith," she said, when he growled.

"Anything is better as long as it's with you, Mouse," he whispered, gently cupping her face as he slid his tongue in her mouth. They began to slow dance as they kissed until he pulled away, staring into her eyes. Faith was a vibe, a vibe he could he ride out with forever. “You’re ready?”

“Yes,” whispered, staring at him lovingly.

“Then let’s do this. Love locked in… forever.”

The End

Lastly, join my readers group! Come join!

Readers' Group: Lil Drew's Readers Crew
Facebook: Author Tisha "Lil Drew" Andrews
Instagram: author_tisha_andrews
Twitter: @tisha_p12

www.ingramcontent.com/pod-product-compliance
Ingram Content Group UK Ltd.
Pitfield, Milton Keynes, MK11 3LW, UK
UKHW022023190726
13853UKWH00005B/2092